8-95

Five Tales

The translator

Michael Shotton is Lecturer in Russian at the University of Oxford and a Fellow of St Catherine's College. He has written and broadcast on Leskov and other Russian topics.

NIKOLAY LESKOV

Five Tales

Translated with an Introduction by
Michael Shotton

ANGEL BOOKS
LONDON

© Michael Shotton 1984

First published 1984 by Angel Books,
3 Kelross Road, London N5 2QS

British Library Cataloguing in Publication Data

Leskov, N.S.
  Five tales.
  I. Title
  891.73′3[F]   PG3337.L5

  ISBN 0-946162-12-3
  ISBN 0-946162-13-1 Pbk

Produced for the Publisher by
Alan Sutton Publishing Limited, Gloucester
Printed in Great Britain

Contents

Acknowledgments

I wish to record my warm thanks to John Fennell for his help and advice on points of terminology, and for reading the manuscript. Antony Wood has also made many welcome suggestions on points of detail.

My thanks too to my wife, Emma: without her skill in defining the precise tonality of colloquial interjections, and her unravelling of other subtle mysteries of Leskovian dialogue, this translation would hardly have been possible.

M.S.

Introduction

Nikolay Semyonovich Leskov is in all respects an oddity on the literary landscape of nineteenth-century Russia.

He was born in 1831, three years after Tolstoy. His father, the son of a priest, had acquired the status of nobleman by advancement in the civil service. His mother came of impoverished gentry stock. Leskov's patchwork formal education came to an abrupt end at fifteen, when he left school to become a petty government clerk in the Oryol criminal court. He was not, however, cast in the mould of Akaky Akakevich, Gogol's archetypal downtrodden pen-pusher: through observation, through the avid acquisition of all manner of esoteric information, and above all through intensive reading Leskov rapidly became a model of the self-taught man. As with Gorky, his 'universities' were Russian life and the private world of books.

In 1850 he moved to Kiev, where he worked in the army recruiting office. In 1853 he married – disastrously – Olga Smirnova, who made his life a misery for the few years they lived together, slowly lapsed into insanity, and spent the last thirty years of her life in an asylum. In 1857 Leskov abandoned the civil service and entered the employ of Alexander Scott, the son of a British nonconformist migrant, and Leskov's uncle by marriage. Scott, in partnership with another Britisher called Wilkins, ran a huge commercial enterprise involved in estate-management, agriculture, trading and manufacture. As a commercial agent for the firm, Leskov travelled the length and breadth of European Russia. (Autobiographical echoes relating to Scott and this episode in Leskov's life are heard in two stories in this volume – *A Spiteful Fellow* and *An Iron Will*.)

In 1860 he moved to Petersburg and took to journalism. In the intellectual ferment generated by the Emancipation, Leskov flirted briefly with revolutionary and radical ideas, though he had little or nothing in common with the radicals by way of background, intellectual training or political instinct. Misunderstandings over an article which Leskov wrote dealing with the Petersburg fires of 1862 and a further series of clashes with the wilder fringes of the radical movement led to a *volte-face*: for ten years or so Leskov squandered much of his energy and talent on a personal crusade against the nihilists, the major literary manifestation of which were two longwinded polemical novels – *No Way Out (1864)* and *At Daggers Drawn (1871)*.

Despite this, the 1860s saw the beginnings of a literary career which was to continue for over thirty years until Leskov's death in 1895. The critics, with the exception of Apollon Grigorev, largely ignored him; in so far as he had any apparent political commitment, it was the wrong one for them; and in so far as he had none, he was equally abhorrent. The reading public, however, gave nearly everything he wrote an enthusiastic welcome. Of his longer works, those generally most highly esteemed are *Cathedral Folk* (1872), *The Sealed Angel* (1873), *The Enchanted Wanderer* (1873), *An Iron Will* (1876) and *The Hare's Form* (published posthumously in 1917). The more famous of the shorter pieces, apart from those in the present volume, are *The Musk-Ox* (1863), *Lady Macbeth of the Mtsensk District* (1865; used by Shostakovich as the basis for an opera), *The Lefthander* (1881) and *The Sentry* (1887).

Given that Tolstoy could find no greater fault in Leskov than that he had 'too much talent', one is bound to ask why Leskov is, relatively speaking, so little published in Russia and so little known in the West.

The reasons for his neglect in the West and in the Soviet Union are quite different. In Russia he has never quite shaken off the label of 'reactionary', given to him by the radicals of his time who, like all radicals, could tolerate no writer who satirized their excesses or failed actively to propagate their ideas. He is printed rarely and selectively.

The West's failure to recognize in Leskov a truly great writer must, ironically, be attributed largely to that quality of his work which above all endears him to those many Russians who, despite official disfavour and critical neglect, have always loved and admired him – that is, its distinctively Russian flavour.

Tolstoy's cryptic phrase no doubt referred to that undisciplined brilliance – somewhat akin to the effect of a lighted match on a box of fireworks – which is certainly one of the uniquely Russian aspects of his work. But there is more to his Russianness than just that. At its base lies an unrivalled love and knowledge of the minutiae of Russian life. Every curiosity of custom, personality, incident or idiom which he encountered in his travels as a civil servant and a commercial agent was stored away in memory or notebook to await its deployment in his fiction. No writer, except perhaps Gorky, knew Holy Mother Russia 'beneath the fingernails' as did Leskov; and this experience gave shape to that view of Russian life as a rich *pot-pourri* of colour and mystery which informs all his writing. Actuality and the fantastic imaginings of the Russian popular mind combine: the grotesque of folk superstition merges imperceptibly with the extravagant improbabilities of real life.

Look, for instance, at a couple of characteristic items from one of his finest longer works, *Cathedral Folk* (1872): there is the peasant who, peering open-mouthed into a pond, is choked to death by a small pike which leaps from the water and sticks in his throat; and there is the famous delicacy 'enraged burbot soup', prepared from the liver of a burbot which, while still alive, has been thrashed into a rage with birch twigs. Fishy tales? Well, the latter is fully authenticated by Leskov's son: one of Leskov's friends was apparently very fond of the dish. And there is really no reason why the tale of the pike should stick in our throats either.

Extravagance, improbability, the odd, the extreme, the disorderly – these are fundamental components of Leskov's Russia: yet they are, for him, all underpinned by a profound sense of national identity, and a spirituality in which elements of the Orthodox, the heretical and the downright pagan freely combine.

If then the spirit of Russia is the wayward, the undisciplined, the tragi-comic, the absurd, Leskov's works capture this spirit in form as they do in content. Spontaneity seems sometimes to be the very guiding principle of structure and style. His prose travels, one might sometimes think, only where fancy leads it, while Leskov shifts the responsibility for this indiscipline from himself to a fictional narrator, who may be involved in the narrative – as in *A Spiteful Fellow* (1863) and *A Shameless Rascal* (1877), or may be merely a whimsical observer – as in *Chasing Out the Devil* (1879) and *An Iron Will* (1876).

In the longer works – not represented in this slender volume – digression is often, paradoxically, of the essence. If Tolstoy's novels incurred Henry James's withering description 'loose baggy monsters', Leskov's superbly anarchic pieces might have caused that writer an apoplectic fit. The shorter, however, the tauter. Only occasionally in the present collection is the narrative given free rein: towards the end of *An Iron Will*, for instance, Leskov finds irresistible the knockabout potential of the discovery of a 'devil' in Marya Matveyevna's house; the central narrative is abandoned while Leskov enjoys his new source of fun.

In theme, and particularly in his treatment of the 'issues of the day', Leskov displayed the same colourful unpredictability. When it came to addressing those topics which preoccupied the intellectuals of his time, he contrived regularly to face both ways, either simultaneously or in sequence. His satirical assaults on nihilists and feminists outraged the radicals of the 1860s. The violent anti-clericalism of such pieces as *Snippets from Episcopal Life* (1878–9) succeeded equally in alienating conservative opinion, and cost him his job in a government ministry. Yet elsewhere a bespectacled lady radical or a humane and downtrodden Russian priest will be unblushingly endowed with heroic status.

The fact is that 'issues' interested him hardly at all. Unlike his great contemporaries Tolstoy, Dostoyevsky and Turgenev, Leskov, until his almost accidental embroilment with the nihilists, had taken no part in the great social, political and philosophical debates which had dominated Russian intellectual life since the 1860s. Again like Gorky, he both envied and despised those who had walked the university corridors or sat late in smoky students' rooms debating such 'accursed' questions as the meaning of life, the existence of God, and the destiny of Russia. He was a practical man, proud of his knowledge of human nature and of the complexities of Russian life. For him 'man', 'Russia', 'the peasantry' and suchlike were not abstract concepts to be transformed into the stuff of 'novels of ideas': they were real, infinitely complex phenomena, to be experienced, felt and known.

The stuff of Leskov's writing then is the garish tapestry of Russian life, in which threads of vigour and torpor, nobility and brutality, saintly virtue and squalid vice are densely interwoven. His narrative feeds not upon the rhetoric of political debate, but upon legend, myth, popular idiom, drunken braggadocio, and that imaginative and creative form of fibbing which the Russians call *vran'yo*. At the heart of his style lies the vernacular, in all its colour. Popular idiom, pun, malapropism, dialectism, the comical deployment by ordinary men of the language of learning or of Holy Writ – such are the components of common speech that Leskov uses to wonderfully comic effect. The memorable drunkard and sage Zhiga, in *An Iron Will*, is a superb exponent.

Yet for all that, there is one recurrent, even dominant, theme in Leskov, to which he turns time and time again. Indeed, there is hardly a piece in which it does not at least lurk close beneath the surface. I refer to his measuring of what we might term 'the Russian principle' against the culture and attitudes of Western

Europe. Two stories in this collection – *An Iron Will* and *A Spiteful Fellow* – centre specifically upon this theme. And though it may not be immediately apparent, *The Robber* (1862) bears implicitly upon it too. As for *A Shameless Rascal* and *Chasing Out the Devil*, they are among the finest examples of Leskov's half-earnest, half-ironic celebration of the Russian character.

The typical Russian in Leskov is always memorable if not always good. Leskov's celebration of *simple* men, whether cross-eyed gunsmiths, rebellious peasantry, or wealthy merchants, reflects his failure to find virtue in officialdom, intelligentsia or gentry, and a profound sympathy too for those kept down by poverty, vodka and the lash. At times we might suspect Leskov of doing what so many of his great contemporaries did – perversely defending the backwardness of Russia by finding in her semi-barbarism a mystic superiority over the bourgeois civilization of the West. Yet in fact, despite his undisguised affection for the 'broad nature' of his compatriots, he rarely treats their rough virtues without some measure of irony. We are made perfectly aware that the peasants in *A Spiteful Fellow* are idiotically and self-destructively obstinate, that the philosophizing commissary in *A Shameless Rascal* is indeed a disgusting pig, or that Safronych, who carries the day for Russia in *An Iron Will*, is a coward, a drunkard and a rogue.

Leskov's Russian 'hero' is moved by instinct and conscience, not by reason. He is often submissive and pursues his destiny through sacrifice; yet he may also be violently self-assertive. He is rarely moral in any conventional sense: he may fornicate or even kill; he is almost bound to drink; he may play the *bogatyr* or the feckless layabout. He may be skilled in some esoteric craft, or his talent, like that of Father Flavian in *An Iron Will*, may lie in the art of eating pancakes. But whatever else he is, he is never mediocre and he is never dull.

When the merchant Ilya Fedoseyevich in *Chasing Out the Devil* dispels his *taedium vitae* by a prodigious orgy, followed by a ritual of physical and spiritual purgation, the narrator sees in this a demonstration of the 'good honest faith of the people', a 'falling and rising again' which translates the myth of the resurrection into the terms of everyday life. The rapacious, gluttonous commissary of *A Shameless Rascal* seems to sum it all up well enough: every Russian, he asserts, is capable of great virtue or great vice; which of the two paths he follows depends entirely upon the circumstances in which he chances to find himself.

In measuring the 'Russian' against the 'European' Leskov drew heavily upon personal experience. The narrator figure in *An Iron Will*, and the firm for which he works, directly reflect the author's experience as a commercial agent in the employ of his uncle Alexander Scott. Similarly, Mr Denn, the English steward in *A Spiteful Fellow*, and the Prussian engineer Hugo Pectoralis in *An Iron Will* are both modelled on people Leskov knew. It is a significant point, for it illustrates again that fundamental difference between Leskov and his more famous contemporaries. If the latters' polemics on the topic of 'Russia and the West' tended to be conducted on an abstract theoretical plane – often based on a minimal personal experience not only of Europe but of much of Russia too – Leskov observed and recorded the European mentality and outlook, as it manifested itself in specific individuals and in actual Russian situations. The contest is conducted not through rhetoric, but through human contact.

The subject intrigued and delighted Leskov, providing him with the basis for stories which were hilarious (*An Iron Will*) and often poignant too (*A Spiteful Fellow*). Leskov never falls into the conventional maximalist traps. Just as he surveys with an ironic eye that Russianness which manifests itself in idleness, drunkenness and pig-headedness, so he resists seeing Europeans as all cut from the same cloth. He has no sympathy for the hysterical Slavophile view of the European as the incarnation of atheism, materialism, rationalism and all the other demonic –isms which threatened to subvert the spiritual purity of Holy Russia.

True, Hugo Pectoralis in *An Iron Will* is in many ways simply a projection of prevailing Russian phobias about the 'Prussian' (the idiotically exaggerated nature of which should perhaps remind us of present Western attitudes towards the Russian!) But that does not prevent Leskov's narrator – acting, no doubt, on his creator's behalf – from feeling a twinge of compassion for this smug, obstinate, but essentially honest and innocent man, as the iron in him is relentlessly eaten away by, and finally succumbs to, Russian rust.

It is the British, however, who most often carry the standard for Europe in Leskov's works, and on the whole they are given a very favourable press. True, even the sturdy qualities of the British commonly find themselves upstaged or thwarted by Russian skills, Russian wiles, or sheer Russian stupidity. *An Iron Will*, *A Shameless Rascal*, and above all *A Spiteful Fellow* all touch upon the subject in varying degree. Those wishing to pursue the theme in Leskov should turn next perhaps to *The Lefthander* and *The Sealed Angel*.

The Robber, which has not previously been translated into English, may seem not to be amongst the most typical of Leskov's works, if only because in this early piece narrative is entirely subordinated to other things. However, as an exercise in the close and sympathetic observation of Russian life, in the humane, but never sentimental, depiction of the Russian peasantry, and in the evocation of atmosphere, it is a minor masterpiece. Chekhov, one imagines, would have enjoyed it enormously, not only for its delicate sense of atmosphere and quietness of tone, but also for its subtle questioning of conventional ('bourgeois',if you like) values and attitudes, when seen in the context of real human experience. It is a measure of Leskov's genius that this story was practically his first exercise in creative literature.

Chasing Out The Devil

I

The ritual of *chasing out the devil* can be observed nowhere else than in Moscow, and then only if you have particularly good luck and special patronage.

I witnessed it from beginning to end thanks to a fortunate concurrence of circumstances, and I wish to record it for the benefit of those who really know and love the serious and sublime aspects of our national customs.

Although on my father's side I come of gentry stock, on the other side I am close to the 'people': my mother's family were merchants. She came of a wealthy household, but fell in love with my father and eloped with him. My late father was a ladies' man, and if he set his cap at a girl, usually got his way. So it was with mama, but her parents paid him back for his artfulness by giving her nothing, apart, that is, from a trousseau, some bed linen and the wish that God might show her mercy – all of which she received together with their forgiveness and eternal blessing. My folk lived in Oryol, poorly but proudly, asking no favours of their rich relations on my mother's side, indeed having nothing to do with them at all. However, when the time came for me to go to university, mama began to urge me:

'Do go and visit Uncle Ilya Fedoseyevich, and send him my greetings. Don't think of it as an indignity; one should respect one's elderly relatives, and he is my brother, a devout man, and a man of weight in Moscow. He is unfailingly hospitable – always goes out first to meet his guests with a dish of bread and salt or an icon, and he has been received by the Governor-General in the company of the Metropolitan . . . There's all sorts of useful lessons you could learn from him.'

Now at that time I had just been studying Metropolitan Filaret's *Catechism** and didn't believe in God; but still, I loved my mother and one day got to thinking: 'Here I've been in Moscow for about a year already, and I still haven't done as she asked; I'll go straight away and make myself known to Uncle Ilya Fedoseyevich, give him my mother's greeting, and find out exactly what he can teach me.'

I had learned as a child to respect my elders, especially those who hobnobbed both with the Metropolitan and with Governor-Generals.

So I roused myself, brushed myself down, and set off to visit Uncle Ilya Fedoseyevich.

II

It was somewhere around six in the evening. It was a warm, soft, greyish sort of day – in other words, the weather was good. My uncle's house is well-known – it's one of the grandest in all Moscow, and everybody knows it. I alone had never been there, nor had I ever seen my uncle, even from a distance.

Still, I marched along bravely enough, reckoning that if he received me – fine, and if he didn't – who cared?

I entered the courtyard: by the front door horses were waiting, regular lions of horses, jet-black, with flowing manes and coats shining like the finest satin; they were harnessed to a carriage.

I climbed the steps to the porch and said my piece: nephew, student, kindly announce to Ilya Fedoseyevich, etc. The servants replied: 'The master will be down himself in a moment: he is going for a drive.'

There emerged a very simple, Russian figure of a man, but rather grand; his eyes were very like my mother's, but the

* Asterisks refer to the Notes beginning on page 186.

expression was quite different – very much that of what is known as 'a man of weight'.

I introduced myself. He heard me out in silence, quietly gave me his hand and said: 'Get in, let's take a drive.'

My first instinct was to refuse, but I somehow faltered and got into the carriage.

'To the park!' he ordered.

Our 'lions' immediately jerked forward and set off briskly, setting the back of the carriage gently bouncing up and down: when we left the city behind, they broke into an even sharper pace.

We sat without exchanging a word, but I noticed that my uncle had tipped his top-hat forward over his forehead, and his face wore the sort of pained expression one associates with acute boredom.

He kept looking about him, then fired a glance at me, and out of the blue said:

'I've lost all taste for life.'

I could think of no reply to that, so kept silent.

We drove on. I thought: 'Where is he taking me?' I began to get the feeling that I had perhaps chanced upon something very interesting.

My uncle meanwhile, as though he had suddenly seen a light, began firing a series of rapid orders at the coachman:

'To the right; now left. Pull up by the Yar!'

Before my eyes, the staff of the restaurant poured out to meet us, and began bowing and scraping before my uncle. He, without stirring from his seat, sent for the proprietor. Someone ran off to fetch him. A Frenchman appeared, likewise oozing respect. My uncle, still without stirring, tapped his teeth with the ivory knob of his cane and said:

'How many outsiders?'

'Thirty or so in the dining rooms,' replied the Frenchman, 'and three private rooms are in use.'

'Get rid of the lot of them!'

'Yes, sir.'

'It's now seven,' said my uncle, glancing at his watch. 'I'll be back at eight. Will you be ready?'

'No,' came the reply. 'Eight will be difficult . . . many of them have ordered . . . but if you would care to come back at nine, the whole restaurant will be cleared.'

'Good.'

'What shall I provide?'

'Gypsies, of course.'

'And?'

'An orchestra.'

'One?'

'Better two.'

'Shall I send for Ryabyka?'

'Of course.'

'French ladies?'

'No!'

'Wines?'

'The lot.'

'And food?'

'Give me the menu!'

The *carte du jour* was handed to my uncle.

He studied it, apparently without understanding a word, or maybe he had no wish to understand. He tapped the menu with his cane and said:

'All of it – for a hundred persons.'

With that, he rolled up the menu and tucked it into his caftan.

The Frenchman, despite his delight, hesitated.

'I can't manage everything for a hundred people. Some of the dishes are so expensive that I don't have enough in the restaurant for more than five or six portions.'

'Well, you can't expect me to treat some of my guests differently from others. Give all of them what they want. Understood?'

'Understood.'

'Otherwise, my friend, even Ryabyka won't be able to do anything about it. Drive on!'

Our carriage rolled off, leaving the proprietor and his staff standing at the door.

At this point I became finally convinced that I was completely out of my depth, and made a half-hearted effort to take my leave; but my uncle wasn't listening. He was very preoccupied. As we drove along we kept stopping people, one after the other; to each of them my uncle said briefly: 'Nine o'clock at the Yar.' And every single person he said this to – respectable-looking old fellows, the lot of them – doffed his hat and replied, equally laconically: 'Delighted, Fedoseyich, delighted.'

I don't recall precisely how many people we stopped in this way – about twenty, I should think – by which time it was nine o'clock and we were rolling up to the Yar once again. A whole crowd of servants tumbled out to meet us: they gave my uncle an arm on both sides, while the Frenchman waited in the porch to brush the dust from his trousers with a napkin.

'Have they all gone?' my uncle asked.

'There's one general,' the restaurateur replied, 'who's a bit slow, and has specially asked to be allowed to finish his meal in his private room.'

'Out with him at once!'

'He'll finish very soon.'

'I don't want him here; I gave him time enough, he can go and finish eating out on the grass.'

It's hard to say how this might have ended: fortunately, at that moment the general emerged, accompanied by two ladies, got into a carriage and drove off, just as the guests to whom my uncle had issued invitations in the park began to arrive at the door.

III

The restaurant was clean, tidy, and empty of clientèle. In one of the rooms, however, a giant of a man was sitting; he greeted my uncle without a word, took his cane, and put it away somewhere.

My uncle surrendered the cane without demur, and at the same time handed over to the giant his wallet and his purse.

This massive, greying figure was none other than Ryabyka, the subject of my uncle's order to the restaurateur – an order which at the time I did not understand. By profession Ryabyka was some sort of 'schoolteacher', but he clearly had some particular function here too: he was every bit as necessary as the gypsies, the orchestra and the rest of the paraphernalia, which had appeared as if by magic, and complete to the last detail. I couldn't fathom the role of this schoolteacher, but I still had a lot to learn.

The brightly lit restaurant was abuzz with activity: music blared, gypsies strolled about, picking up drinks and a bite to eat from the buffet. My uncle was inspecting the dining rooms, the garden, the grotto and the gallery, looking for 'outsiders'. With him went his inseparable companion, the schoolteacher. When they returned to the main hall, however, where the guests were assembled, it was easy to detect a considerable difference between them: their tour of the premises had not affected them equally: for whereas the teacher was as sober as when they had set out, my uncle was completely drunk.

How this could have happened so quickly is a mystery: still, my uncle was in fine spirits. He sat down in the place of honour and the festivities began.

The doors were locked, and as far as the outside world was concerned the order was given: 'Let no man cross thence hither, nor thither hence'. Between the outside world and ourselves a chasm yawned – a chasm of abundance, of wine and food, above all of revelry; I do not mean debauch, but wild, furious revelry, such as I cannot find words to describe. It would, in any case, be pointless to ask that of me, since, seeing myself trapped here in isolation from the world, I took fright and hastened to get drunk too. I will therefore give no account of the events of that night, because it is beyond the power of my pen to describe it all; I recall only two moments of the battle and its finale – but it was these moments that largely accounted for the sense of awe I felt.

IV

Someone came to say that a certain Ivan Stepanovich was at the door – I subsequently discovered that he was one of Moscow's leading factory-owners and merchants.

This caused a slight interruption.

'I said, did I not, that no one was to be admitted,' was my uncle's response.

'His honour is very insistent.'

'Tell him to clear off back to wherever he came from.'

The servant went away, but timidly returned.

'Ivan Stepanovich,' he said, 'asked me to tell you that he begs you most humbly to admit him.'

'No, I don't want him.'

One or two of the others said: 'Let him pay a fine.'

'No, send him packing. I'm not interested in fines.'

The servant came back once more and even more timidly announced:

'His honour is prepared to pay any fine you like: it's just that his honour says it's very sad for him, at his age, not to keep pace with his fellows.'

My uncle rose to his feet, eyes flashing. At this moment Ryabyka also stood up, towering between my uncle and the servant. With his left hand he tossed the latter to one side, as though plucking a feather from a chicken; with his right hand he eased my uncle back on to his chair.

From among the guests voices were raised in support of Ivan Stepanovich: they asked that he be admitted on payment of a hundred roubles for the musicians.

'The old fellow is one of us, he's a pious man, how can we turn him away? He might feel rejected and cause a scene in front of the common folk. We should take pity on him.'

My uncle listened carefully and said:

'If it can't be done my way, it won't be done your way either. Let it be done God's way. I'll let Ivan Stepanovich in, but only if he plays the kettle-drum.'

A messenger was despatched and returned with the words:

'His honour asks that you should rather make him pay a fine.'

'He can go to the devil! If he won't play the drum, it's up to him – he can clear off wherever he pleases.'

It wasn't long before Ivan Stepanovich gave in and sent to say that he agreed to play the kettle-drum.

'Let him in.'

The man who entered was trying hard to put on an imposing and dignified air. His appearance was austere, his eyes lacklustre, his back bent, his beard unkempt and streaked with green. He made as if to exchange greetings and pleasantries with the company, but was quickly checked.

'Later, later, we'll have that later,' my uncle shouted at him, 'but now, beat your drum.'

'Beat your drum!' the others chorused.

'Give us some music – for the kettle-drum!'

The orchestra struck up something noisy. Our stately old man took up the wooden drumsticks and began beating the kettle-drum, half in time, half out of time with the music.

The shouting and the din were positively infernal. The whole company was yelling in delight:

'Louder!'

Ivan Stepanovich did his best to drum harder.

'Louder, louder, still louder!'

The old man hammered for all he was worth, like the Moorish king in Freiligrath's poem,* and finally things reached their desired climax. The drum emitted a desperate rending sound, the drumskin split, everyone burst into laughter, the din reached unimaginable proportions, and Ivan Stepanovich was fined five hundred roubles to compensate the musicians for the ruined drum.

He paid up, wiped his mouth, and sat down. Only then, as everyone was drinking his health, did he notice, to his considerable dismay, that his own son-in-law was sitting among the guests.

The laughter and the din started up again and went on until I finally drifted into a stupor. I remember in my few lucid moments seeing the gypsy girls dancing, and my uncle sitting in his chair, jerking his legs in time to the music. Then he got up to confront someone, but the figure of Ryabyka immediately rose to separate them, and someone was sent flying, and my uncle sat down, while in front of him two forks stood with their prongs driven into the table-top. I now understood what Ryabyka was there for.

Then at last the freshness of a Moscow morning was wafting in through the window, and I returned vaguely to consciousness, though, it seemed, only in order to question whether I had lost my reason entirely. A battle was in progress, a forest was being felled: I heard a cracking and a crashing; trees were swaying, exotic virgin forests, while behind them swarthy faces huddled together in a corner; near me, down at the roots, there was the terrifying gleam of axe blades; my uncle was chopping, the old man Ivan Stepanovich was chopping . . . A scene straight from the Middle Ages.

What was happening was that the gypsy girls, who had hidden behind the trees in the grotto, were being 'taken captive'. Their menfolk were not defending them, but had left them to their own devices. How much of this was in fun and how much in earnest, I could not tell: plates, chairs, and stones from the grotto were flying through the air, while the wood-choppers continued with their frenzied labours, with Ivan Stepanovich and my uncle hacking away even more zealously than the rest.

At last the fortress fell: the gypsy girls were seized, embraced, smothered in kisses: each captor stuffed a hundred-rouble note into his captive's corsage – and that was the end of the affair.

Yes; suddenly everything went quiet . . . it was all over. There was nothing to stop it going on, but they had had enough. Just as they had felt that, without this, 'they had no more taste for life', so now they felt satisfied.

There had been plenty for everyone, and everyone had had his fill. The fact that the teacher announced that it was 'time for school' might also have had something to do with it – but then, perhaps it didn't. Walpurgis-night had passed, and life could now begin to be lived again. The guests did not take their leave and go their separate ways, they simply vanished. The musicians and the gypsies had already gone. The restaurant was a total wreck; no drape was untorn, no mirror intact, even the central chandelier lay shattered on the floor, where its cut-glass prisms were trodden beneath the dragging feet of the exhausted servants. My uncle sat alone in the middle of a sofa, drinking kvass. Every now and then some memory of the night would come back to him and his legs would twitch. Beside him stood Ryabyka, waiting to hurry off to school.

The bill was presented: it was short and all-inclusive.

Ryabyka studied it carefully and demanded a reduction of fifteen hundred roubles. After a brief argument, they arrived at a total of seventeen thousand roubles. Ryabyka, maintaining his watching eye, pronounced it fair. My uncle said curtly: 'Pay!', put on his hat and with a nod motioned to me to follow him.

To my dismay I saw that he had forgotten nothing, and there was no hiding from him. I was absolutely in awe of him, and could not imagine how I might remain alone in the company of this man in his present state of euphoria. He had taken me along with him without a word of explanation, now he was dragging me off somewhere else and I couldn't get away. What would become of me? Even my Dutch courage had now completely evaporated. I was, quite simply, afraid of this dreadful wild beast with his extravagant fancies and terrifying energy. In the meantime, we were about to leave. In the lobby we were besieged by a crowd of lackeys. My uncle ordered: 'Five each', and Ryabyka paid out the money. The yard-porters, watchmen, constables and members of the gendarmerie who had rendered us some service were also paid, though a smaller sum. All these demands were satisfied: but it added up to a tidy sum, and out in the park, as far as the eye could see, the coachmen were waiting. There were colossal numbers of them, and they too were waiting for us, waiting for the good gentleman Ilya Fedoseyevich 'in case his honour should require anything to be fetched'.

They were counted, and the sum of three roubles for each of them was handed over. My uncle and I then got into our carriage, and Ryabyka handed back my uncle's wallet.

Ilya Fedoseyevich took out a hundred-rouble note and handed it to Ryabyka.

He turned the note over in his hands and said curtly: 'Too little.'

My uncle added two more twenty-fives.

'It's still not enough: remember, there wasn't a single ugly scene.'

My uncle added another twenty-five, whereupon the teacher handed him his cane and, with a bow, took his leave.

V

Left to each other's company, we dashed back towards Moscow, while behind us the rag-tag gang of coachmen whooped and rattled along at breakneck speed. I couldn't fathom what it was they wanted, but my uncle knew well enough. It was an outrage: they hoped he would hand over another tip, just to persuade them to go away; and so, under the guise of doing Ilya Fedoseyevich special honour, they were deliberately exposing his most worshipful person to public humiliation.

Moscow lay immediately before us in full view. It lay bathed in the glorious morning light and the fine haze of chimney smoke, through which came the peaceful sound of church bells, summoning the faithful to prayer.

On both sides of the road, stretching up to the city gates, stood rows of chandlers' shops. My uncle pulled up at the first of them, walked over to a limewood tub standing by the entrance and asked:

'Honey?'

'Yes.'

'How much for the tub?'

'We sell it loose, by the pound.'

'Well, sell me the lot. Work out the price.'

As I recall, it came out at about seventy or eighty roubles.

My uncle casually handed over the money.

Meanwhile our cortège had caught up with us.

'Well, my fine lads, coachmen of this city, and do you love me?'

'How can you ask, sir? We are always at your honour's . . .

'And do you have warm feelings for me?'

'We do, sir, we do.'

'Then take off your wheels.'

They stared at him in bewilderment.

'Come on, come on!' my uncle ordered.

The sharper ones, some twenty of them or so, jumped down, fished out spanners from under the coach-box and began loosening the wheel nuts.

'Right,' said my uncle, 'now smear the axles with honey.'

'But sir!'

'Get on with it!'

'To use such good stuff . . . it would be better to put it in our mouths.'

'Get on!'

Without further ado, my uncle got back into our carriage and we charged off again, while the coachmen, the whole gang of them, were left with their wheels off, standing over a tub of honey – which they doubtless did not use to grease the axles, but either divided up amongst themselves, or sold back to the chandler. In any case, we were rid of them, and promptly drew up at the public baths. I thought my end had come; I sat immersed in a marble bathtub, more dead than alive. My uncle meantime had stretched himself out on the floor, not in the simple way men ordinarily lie, but in a pose which had something of the apocalyptic about it. The enormous bulk of his massive frame was entirely supported upon the very tips of his fingers and his toes; his pink body, propped up on these slender fulcra, quivered beneath a well-directed spray of icy water; he was making that sort of subdued bellowing noise that is made by a bear when it tries to tear out its nose-ring. This went on for half an hour or so, during which time he continued to tremble all over like a jelly on a wobbly table, until finally he leapt to his feet and demanded some kvass. We dressed and set off for the 'Frenchman's' establishment on the Kuznetsky Most.

Here our hair was lightly trimmed, waved and dressed; we then continued on foot into the city, to my uncle's store.

While all this was going on, he neither spoke to me nor let me from his side. Only once did he break silence to say: 'Be patient, don't expect everything at once. What you don't understand now, you will, as you grow older.'

At the shop, he surveyed all present with a proprietorial eye, prayed awhile, and went to his desk. The outside of the vessel had been cleansed, but inside there still stirred some profound abomination, demanding to be purged.

I saw this, and was no longer afraid. I was intrigued. I wanted to see how he would come to terms with himself – by some act of self-denial or by an act of grace?

At about ten o'clock he became desperately fidgety, waiting and looking out for the owner of the shop next door, so that the three of us could go and take tea together – that way it was five kopecks cheaper. The neighbour did not appear; he had, it emerged, suddenly died.

My uncle crossed himself and said: 'It comes to all of us.'

He was not in the least put out, despite the fact that they had been going to the Novotroitsky tavern together to drink tea for forty years.

He invited the owner of the shop on the other side: during the day we went out several times for a bite to eat, but we did not touch strong drink. I spent the whole day with him, either at the shop or out and about the city: as evening approached, my uncle ordered a carriage to take us to the Vsepetaya icon.*

There too he was immediately recognized and afforded the same respectful welcome as at the Yar.

'I wish to make obeisance before the Vsepetaya and weep for my sins. And this – allow me to introduce him – is my nephew, my sister's boy.'

'Please be welcome,' said the nuns, 'for from whom should the Madonna rather accept penance than from you, who are such a benefactor of this, her cloister? You have chosen the most appropriate time to approach her – for it is vespers.'

'Let it finish. I prefer to be alone: and please be so good as to arrange a reverential darkness for me.'

The lighting was duly dimmed; everything was extinguished except for one or two small icon lamps and the large lamp with a deep green glass base which hung before the Vsepetaya icon itself.

My uncle not so much fell as crashed to his knees, hurled himself prostrate, uttered a single sob, and seemed to lapse into total stillness.

I sat with the two nuns in a dark nook behind the door. Time passed. My uncle lay without either raising his voice in prayer or making any act of contrition. It looked to me as though he had fallen asleep, and I even put this notion to the nuns. The elder sister thought awhile, shook her head, and lit a slender candle. Clutching it in her hand, she stole quietly up to the penitent. After tiptoeing right round him, she whispered excitedly:

'It's working . . . She's turning him.'

'How can you tell?'

She bent down low, motioning to me to do the same, and said:

'Look, just beyond the lamp – look at his legs.'

'Yes, I see.'

'See, what a struggle!'

Straining my eyes, I was indeed able to detect a slight movement. As my uncle lay in his reverential attitude of prayer, his legs resembled two squabbling cats: each in turn would pounce, causing the other to leap into the air.

'Sister,' I said, 'where have those cats come from?'

'It only looks to you like cats,' she replied. 'What you see is not cats, but temptation: you see, his spirit is burning to reach heaven, while his feet are treading the path to hell.'

I could see that my uncle's feet were certainly still dancing the *trepak** of the night before: but was his spirit now burning to reach heaven?

As though in answer to my question, he suddenly heaved a sigh and yelled out:

'I'll not rise to my feet until you forgive me! For thou alone art holy, while we are accursed devils!' – and he burst into sobs.

So heartfelt was this sobbing that the three of us began sobbing too: 'Oh Lord, do unto him as he beseecheth!'

We failed to notice that he was already standing next to us, saying to me in a low, devout voice: 'Come on, it's time to take our leave.'

The nuns enquired: 'And were you so privileged as to see the holy radiance?'

'No,' he replied, 'I was not so honoured, but it was . . . like this.'

He clenched his hand and raised it, as one would pull a small boy to his feet by his hair.

'You were raised?'

'I was.'

The nuns crossed themselves, as did I. My uncle explained:

'Now are my sins forgiven! Straight from above my head, from the dome of the church His open right hand reached down, took me by the hair, and lifted me straight on to my feet . . .'

No longer did he feel cut off from the world; he was happy. He made a generous gift to the nunnery where his prayer had wrought this miracle: once again he felt the lust for life. He sent my mother the whole of her marriage portion, and as for me – he converted me to the good honest faith of the people.

Since that time I have come to understand the popular urge to fall and rise again . . . And this is that mystery which is known as *chasing out the devil* 'which casteth out the demon of discontent'. I must repeat, however, that one may have the honour of witnessing it nowhere else than in Moscow, and then only if one is particularly lucky, or if one enjoys the special patronage of the city's most dignified elders.

A Spiteful Fellow

As told by an official in the Special Assignments Department

I

When the previous governor was in charge of the province, there was no smoking allowed in our office. Senior staff used to go for a smoke to a little room tucked away behind the head of department's office; juniors had to use the caretaker's cubby-hole. This 'popping out for a smoke' would account for a good half of the working day. I and my colleagues in the Special Assignments Department didn't have to sit in the office all day, so we had no real need of these quiet corners: yet there was not one of us who did not consider it his duty to come and help stain with his cigarette smoke the walls of the room behind the boss's office. It served as a meeting place to which we would all hasten for a chat or a gossip, to have a laugh or swap advice.

Once, I was reviewing an enquiry which I had just completed and, having worked myself to a standstill, went out for a breath of fresh air. It was a splendid day, warm, with dripping roofs and puddles at all the crossroads. I dawdled my way over to the office and decided to call in and have a smoke. The boss was out delivering an official report to the provincial governor. In the little room behind his office I discovered his two assistants, the chief of police and one of my colleagues, who had just returned from conducting an enquiry in one of our more remote districts. I managed to shake hands all round, light a cigarette and perch myself on the windowsill without breaking the flow of conversation which had begun before my arrival. My young colleague in

the Special Assignments Department was giving a heated
account of the administrative abuse that he had uncovered in a
certain police department. Actually, there was nothing particularly diverting about what he had to tell, and the person most
interested in the tale was unquestionably its teller, who seemed
to believe that the discovery of malpractice in some branch of
the administration was a first step towards its eradication. One
of the assistant heads of department was still listening in a
desultory way: the other was unceremoniously drumming his
fingers on the window-glass. The chief of police meanwhile,
straddling his cavalry sabre as though it were a horse and
blowing smoke rings from beneath his moustache, looked as
though at any moment he might exclaim: 'What an idiot you
are, my lad!'

II

While we were thus occupied, the connecting door to the boss's
office opened, and we heard his voice saying to someone: 'This
is our clubroom. Why don't you have a smoke? I'll just finish
what I'm doing and then I'll be at your service.'

In the doorway appeared a tall thickset fellow of about forty,
with glasses, fair hair thinning on top and an amiable expression
on his face.

'This is Mr Denn,' said the boss. 'Mr Denn has been appointed by Prince Kulagin, gentlemen, as steward of his estates.
Pray be acquainted. These,' he said, turning to Mr Denn, 'are
my colleagues N, X, Y, and Z.'

There followed a routine exchange of handshakes, punctuated
by 'Delighted! . . . Honoured! . . .' and so on.

The boss disappeared into his office together with the chief of
police, and we resumed our *dolce far niente*.

'Have you been in these parts long?' asked my young colleague, who liked to be thought of as a man of fashion.

'It's my first time in this province,' said Mr Denn. 'In fact I got here only yesterday.'

'Quite. But what I meant was – do you know this province at all?'

'How can I put it . . . I do and yet I don't. I'm familiar with the Prince's estates from the reports which have been made available to me by his main estates office and from what my principal has told me. On the other hand . . . but then I suppose your province is no different from Voronezh Province or Poltava Province, where I have already had charge of estates belonging to the Prince.'

'That's not entirely the case,' said one of the assistant heads of department, who was held to be something of a specialist in political economy.

Denn turned to him. 'In what would you say the particularities of this province find sharpest expression?' he asked. 'I should be most grateful for the benefit of your experience.'

'Oh, in a variety of things.'

'Pray do not misunderstand me, I am not questioning what you say. I would simply care to know what obstacles I may encounter, if in this province I employ the same system of management which I have used since I came to Russia. I am firmly of the opinion that a single system, strictly adhered to, will always achieve the best ends.'

Our tame political economist was unable to reply to this enquiry, because my young colleague interrupted to ask: 'Have you been in Russia long?'

'Six years and more,' answered Denn.

'You are, if I'm not mistaken . . . from foreign parts?'

'I'm English.'

'Yet you speak Russian so well.'

'Oh yes. I studied the language while in England, since when I have been for more than six years in daily contact with the peasantry. My mastery of Russian, then, should occasion no surprise!'

'And have you fully accustomed yourself to our people and our ways?'

'I believe so,' said Denn with a smile.

'The Prince's estates in our province are in rather a poor way.'

'So I have heard.'

'You will have quite a job on your hands.'

'No more so than elsewhere. Nothing is achieved without effort.'

'I suspect you may need more of that commodity here than in other places.'

'That may be so, sir. But all that is required is a method. One should be neither barbaric, nor indulgent. Management should be systematic, firm, unwavering, but rational. There should be method in everything one does.'

'And might I enquire where you intend to take up residence?'

'I have in mind the village of Rakhmany.'

'But why not Zhizhki? That was where the late Princess lived: the house is there, ready to move into, and complete with servants; whereas there is nothing like that in Rakhmany, as far as I know,' my young colleague observed.

'I do have my reasons,' said Denn.

'Your own . . . system,' the boss's assistant interposed with a laugh.

'Precisely.'

The door opened again and the boss, already with his hat on, said to Denn: 'Shall we go, sir?'

We shook hands once more and parted.

III

The village of Rakhmany is a mere stone's throw from the Gostomelsky farmsteads,* where I was born and where my mother still lived. From the village to the farmsteads is barely nine versts,* and nothing goes on in the one that is not quickly known in the other. When in the line of duty I had to visit the district of K., I would always make a detour to the farmsteads to visit my mother and check the state of her rather fragile finances. My mother had already made the acquaintance of Stuart Yakovlevich Denn and his wife, and each time I called, she was ever more unstinting in her praise. For Denn himself her admiration knew no bounds.

'There's a real man for you,' she would say, 'intelligent, efficient, full of common sense. There's order and method in everything he does; he knows how much to spend and how much to keep in hand; in a nutshell, you can see he's no product of our idiotic Russian upbringing!'

His other neighbours doted on Denn likewise. His name had become a veritable byword: 'Denn says that's the way to do it; that's not the Denn way of doing things.' Denn was on everybody's tongue. A whole fund of stories and anecdotes about Denn was already in circulation. Since Stuart Yakovlevich's arrival, they said, everything had been turned upside down on the Prince's estates; he'd really set the cat among the pigeons. He had found a place in his scheme of things even for incorrigible thieves, of whom there was no particular shortage in our area. Not only that: the most notorious loafers he had made overseers; thieves who had seen the inside of a gaol on more than one occasion he had put in charge of accounts, entrusted with the keys of the stores and set to mind the village shop – and all to such good effect that he was the envy of the whole district. 'Well, well,' I thought to myself, 'we've actually found a man who knows how to handle the peasants!'

I was keen to go and observe the miracles being performed in Rakhmany, but I never seemed to get the opportunity. Meanwhile, the year slipped by and winter returned.

IV

On the evening of the fourth of December a police messenger brought a note summoning me later that evening, at eleven o'clock, to the provincial governor.

When, in response to the note, I entered the governor's presence, he asked me: 'You were born in these parts, I believe?'

I said yes, that was so.

'You lived for some time in the K. district?'

'I spent my childhood there,' I said. 'The K. district is my native heath.'

'And do you know many people there?' the governor pursued his questioning.

'What the devil . . .?' I thought, weathering the interrogation, and answered that there was hardly a soul in the district I did *not* know.

'I have a request to make of you,' the governor said. 'Prince Kulagin writes from Paris to inform me that he has despatched to his estates in this area an Englishman called Denn, an experienced man, and one who has rendered the Prince excellent service for some considerable time. Yet the Prince is deluged with complaints about him. I beg you – not as a duty, but as a favour – visit the district, get to the root of the matter as best you can, so that I in my turn may do what is for the best.'

I set off for the district town of K. that same night, and was at my mother's house the next day in time for morning tea. She had heard nothing of the peasants' complaints against Denn. When I asked her if she knew of any trouble with the Rakhmany peasants, she replied: 'No, my dear child, I've heard nothing. In any case, whatever could they find to complain about with Stuart Yakovlevich in charge!'

'Perhaps,' I suggested, 'he is too strict or intemperate?'

'Well, of course, he does like things done properly.'

'Does he maybe use the birch too much?'

'Good heavens, no! He doesn't use it at all! If anyone gets a beating, it's in front of the whole village, by judgement of the *mir**.

'Then perhaps he is not as cautious as he might be in a certain matter. . . ?'

'What are you driving at?'

'Well,' I said, 'does he turn his head when a pretty headscarf goes by?'

'Oh really, have mercy!' my mother retorted, spitting to underline her contempt for the idea.

'Why are you so angry, mama?'

'Well, what nonsense you do talk!'

'Why nonsense? Such things do happen.'

'But he's a married man.'

'Yes, dear mama,' I said, 'but a married man can have more wicked dreams even than a bachelor.'

'Oh, get along with you,' my mother retorted once more, barely concealing a smile.

'Then what is it that he has done to get the peasants' backs up?'

'What, my child! How could he do anything other than get their backs up? Oafs they always were, and oafs they remain. Mischief and thieving – that's all they're good for!'

V

My visits to two or three other houses in the neighbourhood produced the same result. On St Nicholas' Day there was the customary village fair. I called in at the priest's house and attempted in the course of conversation to discover some reason for the peasants' discontent with Mr Denn. Everywhere I got the same reply – that Stuart Yakovlevich was a steward in a million, and as good as a father to the peasants. What was I to do? 'There's no two ways about it,' I thought to myself, 'the peasants must be lying.' I had no choice but to return to the town empty-handed.

When I arrived, I called casually on an old friend of my late father, the merchant Rukavichnikov. I had in mind nothing more than to warm myself with a cup of the old fellow's tea, while my post-horses were being prepared, but he insisted I stay for dinner. 'It's my youngest son's name-day,' he said. 'There's a pie sitting in the oven, and you think I'll let you go! Don't dream of it! I'll just call my good wife and daughters to pay their respects.'

I had no option but to stay.

'Meanwhile, we'll go and take tea,' said Rukavichnikov.

In a room on the mezzanine a fat-bellied samovar was placed before us and my host and I sat down to tea.

'Well, my lad, what brings you to these parts, your own business or somebody else's?' Rukavichnikov enquired, after we had made ourselves comfortable and he had set the tea to brew and draped a white cloth over the teapot.

'You could say – both, Pyotr Ananich,' I answered.

I knew Pyotr Ananich as a shrewd and modest man, who moreover knew the whole district like the back of his hand.

'Actually,' I said, 'it's a silly sort of business, but tricky too,' and I told him for what purpose I had come.

Pyotr Ananich listened attentively and smiled once or twice in the course of my tale: when I finished, he merely commented: 'Tricky your business may be, but silly – no.'

'Do you know Denn, then?'

'Good heavens, how could I not know him?'

'And what do you think of him?'

'Well, what *can* one think of him?' the old man pronounced with a helpless gesture. 'He's a good master.'

'Good?'

'There's no question about it.'

'Is he fair?'

'I've heard no word against him in that respect.'

'Too strict, perhaps?'

'Not in the slightest.'

'Then what are the complaints about?'

'How can I put it? He's a very good man . . . he could do with being a little less so . . . that's what lies at the base of the complaints. The peasants just can't stomach him.'

'How do you mean, can't stomach him?'

'He wants things done in an orderly way . . . orderly, you understand, and we find that hard to bear.'

'Perhaps he overburdens them with work?'

'Overburdens them, heavens no! Their life's twice as easy as it used to be . . . But . . . wait a minute, look, there's one of the Rakhmany peasants just trudged into town for some reason or other. Eh! Filat! Filat!' Rukavichnikov yelled through the window. 'Now you'll hear a tale or two,' he added, shutting the window and sitting down again at the table.

Up into the room where we were sitting came a short, dim-sighted muzhik with tiny purulent eyes: he proceeded to cross himself before the icons.

Rukavichnikov waited until he had finished, then said, 'Good day to you, Filat Yegorych!'

'Good day, Pyotr Ananich sir.'

'And how is life treating you?'

'Eh?'

'How are you getting along, I say?'

'Praise God, we still keep body and soul together.'

'And is everything well with you at home?'

'Not so bad, Pyotr Ananich, not so bad.'

'Nothing to complain about?'

'Eh?'

'Anything to complain about, I say?'

'Eh-hey. Why should we have nothing to complain about?'

'Well, what's the matter then?'

'Akh, God alone knows. It's like . . . life ain't free any more.'

'Is it the steward again?'

'And who else might it be?'

'What's he done to hurt your feelings this time?'

'He's got it into his head to build a factory.'

'Well?'

'So he won't release us to go and earn money in the Ukraine.'

'What, no one?'

'He hasn't let a single carpenter go.'

'That's not good.'

'What good would you expect of him? We sent off a complaint to the Prince, our master: two *pestitions* we sent, but we still ain't had no answer.'

'Dear, dear, you have fallen on evil days and no mistake,' Rukavichnikov remarked.

'Ugh, that brute, he makes us suffer.'

Rukavichnikov turned to me. 'There now, you see what a scoundrel your friend Denn is!' he said.

The muzhik turned his gaze to me.

'And now I'll tell you something else,' my host continued. 'Now I'll tell you what a scoundrel this Filat Yegorych here is.'

At this, our muzhik did not bat an eyelid.

'Mr Denn, their steward, is a man as kind-hearted and as fair as they come . . .'

'True enough, that is,' the peasant interrupted.

'Yes. Yet this same Mr Denn can't get on with the peasants. He's for ever introducing his own way of doing things: but, as I see it, it's not a question of different ways of doing things; it's simply that he's too weak.'

'Weak, aye, that's the measure of it,' the peasant echoed once more.

'Quite. He's been there over a year, and I ask you – has he so much as laid a finger on any of them? Well, is it true what I say?'

'It's true sir, he hasn't.'

'There, you see; they don't like that. When he does punish someone, it's something mild – and as often as not he doesn't get round to it at all. They all have a fixed amount of work to do, but it's not a heavy load. Do what you have to do, then you're free to do what you like.'

'Aye, that's it, off you go.'

'What?'

'When you've done your job – that's it . . . off you go, wherever you please,' the peasant repeated.

'Exactly. And then, would you believe it, the next minute they're writing complaints about him.'

Filat Yegorych said nothing.

'Why then doesn't he release them to go and earn some money?' I said.

'He doesn't, it's true. But why don't you enquire of our friend Filat Yegorych here how much that fine son of his, who has been away two years earning money, has brought back home? Come on, Filat Yegorych, why don't you tell us?'

The peasant stood stubbornly silent.

'Well, I'll tell you what his son brought back with him: a Ukrainian bag containing a broken English plane; and to his wife and children a small gift of French origin, the result of which can be observed in the collapsed noses of nearly all the family. Well, is it the truth I tell?' Rukavichnikov addressed the peasant again.

'It were so, sir.'

'Indeed it was. Well now, Stuart Yakovlevich had the idea of building a distillery. I praise him for that; because he doesn't intend to start up some huge industrial monster; he plans just to distil from his own barley and feed his cattle on the grains. He was approached by various contractors who offered to do the entire job for five thousand roubles – but he didn't accept. And why do you think that was?'

'There ain't no way for us to know that,' answered Filat Yegorych.

'Not true, brother; you know full well. He worked out what these contractors were asking for the building work; then he calculated how much you would earn a month working for the contractor, and he offered you a rouble a month more, just so you would have a job here at home, instead of to-ing and fro-ing in search of work.'

'There was some talk of that, it's true.'

'Yes, indeed – and it certainly wasn't a case of "no way of us knowing". And now you can bet they've written to complain that instead of releasing them to do paid work, he is making them sweat blood building the distillery; but somehow they will have omitted to mention the pay they are getting. Is that not so?'

'I don't know nothing o' that.'

'Just as I would expect. That's my old friend Filat Yegorych for you! Love him for the splendid fellow that he is!'

The muzhik grinned.

'What you need is me for your steward,' Rukavichnikov went on jokingly. 'How would you like that?'

'Why not, sir?'

'We shouldn't have any squabbles; we should get along famously. We should have a system based on spiritual kinship. If you, Filat Yegorych, got up to any of your tricks, I'd soon settle your hash. As for any lad caught thieving or up to some other mischief, I'd give his ear a tweak or two; and if anyone came back from the Ukraine with the same thing Filat Yegorych's precious son brought back, I'd put him first in hospital, then I'd give him a spot of treatment with some birch rods, then I'd send him back where he came from. That's the way to do things, eh, Filat Yegorych?'

'Aye sir, that's our way.'

'There, you see, I'm a knowing fellow.'

We sent the peasant on his way.

'A fine state of affairs this is!' I said to Rukavichnikov.

'Well, you can see for yourself, my good fellow. Mr Denn is a good man, and my advice to him would be to leave this place before they devise some vile trick to get rid of him.'

I gave a detailed account of the affair to the governor, who nearly exploded with rage. He was an administrator himself, and had been delighted beyond words by the arrival in the province of a rural administrator of the quality of Stuart Yakovlevich Denn.

VI

On the Friday of Shrovetide there was a pancake party at the governor's. Practically the whole town was there. While we were seated at the table the duty officer approached and handed the governor an envelope. The governor tore off the seal, read the message and dismissed the duty officer with the words: 'All right!' However, it was quite apparent that something was far from 'all right'.

After the meal the governor had a word or two with his guests, then vanished discreetly into his office with our head of department. A quarter of an hour later I was called to join them. The governor was standing, leaning on his elbows, behind his high desk, while my head of department was using the writing desk.

'We have a nasty business on our hands,' the governor said, turning to me. 'The peasants at Rakhmany are in revolt.'

'Revolt?'

'Read for yourself.'

He took from his high desk and handed to me the paper which had been given to him during the meal. It was a report from the police officer in charge of K. district to the effect that on the previous day the Rakhmany peasants had risen in revolt against their steward, burned to the ground his house, the distillery and the flour mills, and severely beaten and driven from the village the steward himself.

'I'm sending you immediately to Rakhmany,' said the governor, when I had had time to run through the police officer's report. 'I intend to give you open orders to the officer in command of the local Invalid Company.* Take a detachment of men and do whatever is necessary to put down the revolt and identify the ringleaders. Waste no time: I want you on the spot by tomorrow morning, while the trail is still warm.'

'Might I have your permission not to take soldiers with me?' I asked. 'I know everyone there and I hope I can do what needs to be done without soldiers; they would only be a hindrance.'

'As you think best: but take the open orders to the officer commanding the Invalids just in case.'

I bowed and left, and a mere four hours later was drinking tea in the town of K. with the district police officer, who was to accompany me to Rakhmany. From the town to Rakhmany was fifteen versts, and we arrived at night. There was nowhere for us to stay. The steward's house, the estate office, the servants' quarters, the laundry, the workshops – all had been destroyed by fire together with the distillery and the flour mills; over the black heaps of warm ash there still hung occasional wisps of blue smoke from smouldering beams. We set up our quarters in the house of the village elder and sent for the local policeman. He arrived early in the morning and brought with him the Rakhmany peasant Nikolay Danilov, whom he had arrested the previous evening on suspicion of setting fire to the factory and inciting the peasants to revolt.

'What have you found out?' I asked the policeman.

'It was arson, sir.'

'Why do you say that?'

'All the uninhabited buildings caught fire at night and at the same time.'

'Whom do you suspect of the crime?'

The policeman made a gesture with his hands which underlined his expression of complete bewilderment.

'Then on what grounds have you arrested this man?'

'You mean Nikolay Danilov, sir?'

'Yes.'

'Well, sir, on the day of the crime he had been punished by Mr Denn. He used abusive language to Denn and, moreover, that night he remained in the area of the distillery, which was more or less the first building to catch fire.'

'And that's all?'

'Yes, sir. There's nothing else to go on. The peasants are all keeping their mouths shut.'

'Have you questioned anyone?'

'I have made enquiries.'

'And discovered nothing?'

'Not so far.'

At this point the village elder came in and stopped by the door.

'You wish to say something, Lukyan Mitrich?' I asked.

'It's for a favour I've come, your honour.'

'I see. And what favour can "my honour" do for you?'

'The peasants are assembled.'

'And who told you to call them together?'

'They came of their own accord; they want to talk to you.'

'Where are they?'

'Right outside, sir.'

The elder pointed to the window. Outside, facing it, was a huge crowd of peasants of all ages, from young lads to old men. They were standing quietly, with their hats on; a few had sticks.

'Goodness, what a crowd!' I remarked, doing my best not to show alarm.

'All the Prince's people are here,' said the elder.

'Go and tell them, Mitrich, that I'll just put on my coat, then I'll come outside.'

The elder went out.

'Don't go!' said the policeman.

'Why not?'

'Who knows what might happen?'

'Well, it's a bit late now. A wooden door won't save us: if they've come with mischief in mind, they'll find us just as easily here in the house.'

I put on my fur coat and, accompanied by the local policeman, stepped out on the raised porch. There was a stirring in the crowd, hats started to be pulled off, but reluctantly, not all at once, and at the back of the crowd a few hats remained stubbornly in place.

'Good day to you, lads!' I said, taking off my own hat.

The peasants bowed and droned 'Good day' in return.

'Put your hats on, lads, it's cold.'

'No matter,' they droned again, and at the back the last few hats were removed.

'Come on, please put your hats on.'

'We're all right as we are . . . we're used to it.'

'Then I order you to put them on.'

'Well, if you order us . . .'

One or two of them replaced their hats: the remainder then did the same.

I relaxed. I could see I had done the right thing, not bringing the soldiers with me.

By the porch stood a two-horse sledge: in it sat Nikolay Danilov with his feet locked in wooden fetters. He was wearing a knee-length Ukrainian jacket, tied round with string, and a fur hat. He looked to be about thirty-five years of age; with light brown hair, a pointed beard and a timid, anxious expression on his face. For all his generally downtrodden look, his features were serene and not unhandsome – and this despite a bloodied lip and a weal on the left cheek. He was sitting quietly, looking now at me, now at the crowd.

'What is it you want of me, lads?' I asked the assembly.

'Is it you as is come from the governor, sir?' asked a fellow of middle years from the front row.

'It is.'

'Are you an official?'

'I am.'

'From the governor's office?'

'Yes.'

'Well, there's some things as we'd like to say to you.'

'As you wish. I'm listening.'

'No . . . you come down from up there, off that porch. It's you we want to talk to, nobody else.'

Without a moment's hesitation I went down into the crowd, which opened up, engulfed me and closed again behind me, thus cutting me off from the two policemen.

I found myself facing the same peasant who had invited me down into the crowd.

'Now, what do you want to talk about?'

'We asked you to come down here, seein' as you're one of us, from these parts, not an outsider.'

'What did you want to talk about?'

'Well, about the thing that happened here.'

From various parts of the crowd I detected the sound of sighs.

'Why did you drive out the steward?'

'He went away hisself.'

'I should think he did – after you'd beaten him half to death!' There was silence.

'And what will happen now, do you think?'

'It was what we wanted *you* to tell us – what'll happen to us now?'

'Hard labour in Siberia, that's what.'

'Because of the steward?'

'Yes, because of the steward; *and* the burning; *and* the revolt – for all of it together.'

'There weren't no revolt,' one of them muttered.

'Oh, come on, lads, there's no point in denying it,' I said. 'The evidence is in front of you; it speaks for itself. If you try to dig your heels in, there'll be questions and more questions, and you'll end up telling so many lies, you'll tie yourselves in knots. What you should be thinking about is using your wits to make the best of a bad job.'

'That's true enough,' growled a voice or two.

'You're right, it is. And now, good-bye to you. It looks as though there's nothing for us to talk about.'

I touched one muzhik lightly with my hand; he moved aside, and, after him, a path opened up to let me out.

VII

The enquiry began. The first to be questioned was Nikolay Danilov. Before commencing, I ordered that his fetters be removed. He sat down on a bench and watched impassively as the wedges were pulled out, and then with the same apparent lack of concern got to his feet and approached the table.

'Well, Nikolay, old fellow, you have got yourself into a mess, haven't you?' I said.

Nikolay Danilov wiped his nose on his sleeve and said nothing.

'What have you got to say for yourself?'

'What can I say? There ain't nothing to be said,' he uttered in a trembling voice.

'Come on, old fellow, tell us what happened.'

'I don't know nothing about it and I ain't guilty of any of it.'

'Then tell us what you do know.'

'I know nothing except what happened to myself.'

'And what did happen to you?'

'He did as he pleased.'

'Beat you, you mean?'

'No, I didn't say he beat me. He just kept . . . aggravating me.'

'What did he do to you exactly?'

'He shamed me, more than I could bear.'

'How do you mean exactly, *shamed* you?'

'Well, that's his spesherality, that is.'

'Listen, Nikolay, just talk sense, or I'll leave you to take what's coming to you,' I said with a dismissive wave of the hand.

Nikolay thought for a moment, stood for a moment, then said: 'Let me sit down. My legs ache from the fetters.'

'All right. Sit down,' I said, and ordered a bench to be pulled up to the table for him.

'I asked him to release me to find work,' Danilov began. 'Back in the autumn I asked him, along with the other lads; but he wouldn't let us go, not at that time of year. But I just had to go to Chernigov province.'

'What, did somebody there owe you money?'

'No.'

'What then?'

'Something else.'

'Well?'

'Well, he wouldn't let us go. Made us work on the distillery instead. I worked a week, then I went.'

'Where did you go?'

'Where I said.'

'To Chernigov province?'

'Aye.'

'And what did you have to go there for?'

'To drink cheap vodka,' the policeman prompted him.

Nikolay said nothing.

'And what happened then?'

'Well, in Korilevets I got arrested; they brung me back to our town under escort and when they got me here they handed me over to the steward.'

'Without punishment?'

'They punished me first, then they handed me over. He put me straight to work again, and about ten days ago I run off again – to my own village, to Zhogovo. Then the village elder grabbed me, and marched me off back again to the steward.'

'And what did he do then?'

'He ordered me to sit in the corner.'

'In the corner?'

'In the corner, like I say. The lads are working, and I'm sitting doing nothing in the corner of the building in front of everybody. I asked for an axe, so I could get on with some work, but he says, "No, just sit as you are," he says.'

'So did you sit?'

'I run off again.'

'Why?'

'I begged him, I did: "Let me work," I said – but he wouldn't let me. "You sit there," he says, "where everybody can see you. That's your punishment." "If you want to punish me," I says, "then have me flogged," I says. "Sooner that than me sit here for everyone to laugh at." But he wouldn't do it, he wouldn't give me a flogging. When the bell rang for mealtime, the lads went off to dinner, and I did a bunk, but they caught me outside the village.'

'Then what?'

'Then he treated me worse still.'

'How?'

Obviously embarrassed, the muzhik replied: 'I can't tell that.'

'You've got to tell us,' I said.

'He tied me by a thread.'

'How do you mean, a thread?'

'Like I say,' answered Nikolay Danilov in his lilting voice and blushing like a beetroot. 'He had me brought to the distillery and ordered a lackey to bring a gold armchair from the master's house; he put the chair down opposite where the lads were working, on a pile of shavings, and had me sat on it: he pushed a pin into the back of the chair and tied me to it with a thread, just like a sparrow.'

Everyone burst into laughter: indeed, how could one not laugh at the sight of this fully-grown healthy muzhik telling how he was tied down with a thread?

'And did you stay tied like that for long?'

Nikolay Danilov sighed and mopped his face. The mere thought of the thread had been enough to bring him out in a sweat.

'A whole day I sat there, just like a sparrow.'

'And that evening the fires broke out?'

'Night, not evening. About third cock-crow the fire started.'

'How did you find out about the fire?'

'I heard the shouting in the street, that's all.'

'But until the shouting started,' I enquired, 'where were you?'

'At home, by the barn, asleep.'

The answer came in a calm voice, but he didn't look me in the eye as he said it.

'And how did the steward come to be driven out?'

'I don't know nothing about that.'

'You must have seen them laying into him down by the distillery?'

There was no reply.

'Everyone was there, weren't they?'

'Aye, everyone.'

'And no doubt they were all helping to beat him?'

'I suppose so.'

'And you gave him a thump or two as well?'

'No, I never touched him.'

'Then who did?'

'Everybody.'

'But you didn't notice anyone in particular?'

'No, I didn't.'

Nikolay Danilov was taken aside, and we began to question the nightwatchmen, the gangers, members of Danilov's family, his neighbours and all manner of folk. In three days we listened to about a hundred people: if we had taken down each testimony in writing, we should have used a good ream of paper. Fortunately, there was no point, because they all spoke as one man. What the first said, the others repeated in their turn. And what the first said was this: that he knew nothing of what caused the fire; that, yes, possibly it was started deliberately, but *he* had nothing to do with it and had no idea who did, except maybe the steward himself, because he was a spiteful fellow, and had even taken to tying up peasants with a thread, like so many sparrows. What's more, nobody had driven out the steward; on the contrary, he had left of his own free will, because he'd suffered a bit of unpleasantness – during the fire someone had given him a hiding.

'And *who* gave him a hiding?'

'We don't know.'

'Well, *why* did they do it?'

'It must have been because he was so *spiteful*, because he really made our lives a misery – he even took to tying us with a thread, like so many sparrows.'

The remaining ninety-nine testimonies were word-for-word repetitions of this first one, and we recorded them as follows: Ivan Ivanov Sushkin, age forty-three, married, attends confession, no police record. Testified the same as Stepan Terekhov.

VIII

I began to foresee an appalling outcome to the whole affair. After a good deal of reflection, I ordered that Nikolay Danilov be held in custody, and informed the two policemen that I was leaving for the town of O. for three days. When I got there, I consulted with my head of department and we went together to see the provincial governor. We found him taking evening tea, and in a good mood. I gave my report on the affair and, dressing the whole thing up, as best I could, in simple terms, persuaded him that there hadn't really been a revolt, and that if Prince Kulagin were to state his willingness to forgive the peasants, then the whole business of the fire could be suppressed, there would be no official investigation, no carrying out of sentence, no cat o'nine tails, no hard labour – and order and calm would be restored.

The words 'order and calm' were so pleasing to the governor's ear that he walked up and down a bit, thought a bit, pulled his bottom lip up to his nose a bit, and composed a sixty-word telegram to the Prince. The telegram was despatched that same evening, and two days later we received from Paris the Prince's reply, informing us that he was offering an amnesty to the peasants, so that they might collectively beg the forgiveness of Mr Denn and henceforth never dare to complain about him again on any grounds whatsoever.

I returned immediately to Rakhmany with the Prince's amnesty, summoned a village meeting and announced: 'Lads! In a word, the Prince forgives you. I begged mercy on your behalf from the governor; the governor did likewise with the Prince, and here in my hand I have the Prince's forgiveness, so that in your turn you too may ask forgiveness of your steward and henceforth not make any idle complaints about him.'

The peasants began to bow and thank me.

'Well, what about it? You must choose messengers to go to Mr Denn in the town with your confession of guilt.'

'We'll choose somebody.'

'It must be done promptly.'

'We'll send someone today.'

'And after that, no more of your silly tricks.'

'But we're glad of it ourselves! We don't wish him any harm – we just want to be rid of him.'

'What do you mean, rid of him? The Prince assumes that from now on you'll be living in peace and harmony with Mr Denn.'

'Are you saying he'll be coming back?' several voices asked in unison.

'Well, what did you think I meant?'

'So *that's* it! Oh no, we're not having that!'

'But you yourselves wanted to send off messengers to ask his forgiveness, this very day.'

'Aye, we'll ask his forgiveness all right, but we ain't agreeable to his coming back here!'

'Then there'll have to be an official investigation.'

'Well, if that's how it has to be, so be it – but there ain't no way we'll ever get along with him.'

'What nonsense! Come to your senses! Half of you will be sent off to Siberia!'

'No, we're not having him. How are we going to live with a brute like that?'

'How on earth has he been a brute to you?'

'How *hasn't* he been a brute? Tying up a man with a thread, like a sparrow – what does that make him, if it isn't a brute?'

'For heaven's sake, forget that idiotic thread. As if that silly little thing matters! Are you going to tell me that you were better off when the Prince himself was here? Didn't he drive you to your deaths just sweeping his garden paths? And did you enjoy the sight of his fine black horses each time you were taken to the stables to be flogged?'

'That ain't got nothing to do with it. The Prince is our master, it was his right: and he still never did such things to us as that steward did. God a' mercy . . . tying a man with a thread like a sparrow . . . we never suffered nothing like that, not since we were born.'

'Think what you're doing, lads!'

'What is there to think about? We've thought enough already. If he comes back, we might do something worse than we have yet.'

'He won't be doing any more tying up with thread, I give you my word on that.'

'He'll just think up another nasty trick to play on us.'

'Why should he do that?'

'He's such a . . . spiteful fellow, that's why.'

'Enough of this, lads. I've got to take an answer to the governor.'

There was a pause.

'All right, we're ready to ask forgiveness.'

'And you'll take back the steward?'
'We can't do that.'
'Why can't you?'
'He's spiteful.'

Beyond this the peasants of Rakhmany would not budge. The law duly took its course: three were sentenced to penal servitude in Siberia, twelve or so were sent to join a chain gang, the remainder were taken to the district court, flogged, and sent back home.

A Shameless Rascal

We had weathered a squall at sea in a horribly flimsy little tub, though what was wrong with it, incidentally, I didn't understand. When we dropped anchor, the crew set everything to rights in a matter of half an hour; we too shook ourselves into shape, ate a makeshift dinner and found ourselves in quite a celebratory mood.

We were a small company: the skipper, two naval officers, the navigator, together with myself and the old sailor Porfiry Nikitich. We two had been taken on board for friendship's sake, just to get a breath of sea air.

The sense of euphoria we shared at having narrowly escaped disaster loosened our tongues: the foul weather we had been through served as a natural topic of conversation. A variety of even more perilous moments at sea were recalled, and imperceptibly the conversation shifted to the way a man's character is affected by a life at sea. Needless to say, in a company of seafaring men the sea had champions aplenty: to hear us talk, you would have thought the sea to be a panacea for practically all ills, including that shallowness of feeling, thought and character which was the mark of contemporary man.

'Hm!' said old Porfiry Nikitich. 'I see. That's all right then. There's a simple cure for everything. All you have to do is take all those petty-minded landlubbers, put them aboard ships and send them off to sea.'

'Hang on a minute, that's an odd conclusion to draw!'

'What's so odd about it?'

'Well, that isn't what we were saying at all. We were saying that a man's character is formed by a life spent at sea, not that you can produce an instant change in a fellow by simply taking him and shoving him into a sailor's jacket. The idea is obviously ridiculous.'

'Hold on, hold on,' Porfiry Nikitich interrupted. 'Firstly, this isn't an idea I thought up at all. These are the words of a sage, an actual historical person.'

'Oh, to hell with all those Greeks and Romans!'

'Well, for a start, my actual historical sage wasn't a Greek or a Roman at all, but a Russian, and he worked in the government victualling service; moreover, everything he said on this subject was publicly acknowledged at the time by a sizeable and honourable company of men to be a certain and unquestionable truth. Now I, being a good patriot, would like to defend the idea, because it all touches upon the versatility and virtuosity of the Russian character.'

'Couldn't you tell us the story behind this actual historical declaration?'

'If you wish.'

– Having returned to Petersburg after the Crimean War, I turned up one day at the house of Stepan Aleksandrovich Khrulyov* and encountered there a large and motley company: there were military men from all the services, amongst them a few of our lads from the Black Sea Fleet, who'd got to know Stepan Aleksandrovich in the trenches at Sebastopol. I needn't tell you how delighted I was to meet these mates of mine, and we sailors settled ourselves down at a separate table: we were having a yarn and taking a glass of sherry or two. Now what went on at these parties of Khrulyov's was that people mostly played cards, and, what's more, for pretty high stakes – 'chalked wins and losses on the slate, and never let the game abate',* as the poet has it. The gallant Khrulyov – may God rest his soul and his sins not be remembered! – was a man who liked strong sensations: indeed, at that time he couldn't do without them. Well now, we sailors did without cards and got down to a round-the-table debate; I can remember what started the conversation off – it was a book that had just come out called *The Dirty Side of the Crimean War*. It caused quite a sensation at the time; we had all read every last word of it and were pretty hot under the collar as a result. Well, you can understand it. The book dealt with the abuses that lay at the root of most of our recent suffering – suffering that was still very fresh in the memory of all those who had taken part in the defence of Sebastopol; it all touched us on a very raw nerve. Above all else the book exposed the thieving and embezzlement by people in the commissariat and victualling service, thanks to which all of us had time and again tasted the pleasures of hunger and thirst, cold and damp.

Now as you can imagine, the exposure in print of all these dirty goings-on sparked off individual memories in every one of us, and brought to the boil a good deal of simmering resentment: so, naturally enough, we started blowing off steam. It was a very companionable activity: there we sat, vying to think up ever ruder names for those good friends of ours, the commissaries. At this point, the chap sitting alongside me, another of our Black Sea lads, Captain Yevgraf Ivanovich, a graduate of the Nakhimov Naval Academy, an extraordinarily kindly fellow and a bit of a stutterer, grabs me by the knee under the table and goes suddenly all coy . . .

'What on earth can he want?' I think to myself.

'Excuse me, my dear chap,' I say, 'but if you need something a bit private, call a waiter, will you? I'm a visitor here myself, and I don't know where it is.'

But he just stammered something or other and started doing the same thing again. Now I'm the sort of silly fellow who gets all worked up for no reason at all; what's more, I was already fairly steamed up by all these reminiscences, and on top of that I'm terribly ticklish, and there was this Yevgraf Ivanovich, as bold as brass, tickling my knee with his fingers, just like the soft lips of a nuzzling calf.

'Hey, Yevgraf Ivanovich, turn it in, will you?' I say. 'What do you think you're up to? I'm not a woman, you know, for you to play kneesy-kneesy with under the table. You can tell me your feelings out loud.'

At which poor old Yevgraf Ivanovich – what a priceless fellow! – gets even more flustered, and says in a whisper: 'What a sh-sh-shameless fellow you are, Porfiry Nikitich.'

'I don't know about me,' I say, 'it's you that looks more like the shameless one to me. The way you go on, anyone could suspect us of belonging to some pernicious sect or other.'

'How c-c-can you . . . I m-m-mean, really, one sh-sh-shouldn't speak of c-c-commissaries and supply officers like that.'

'And why should you,' I ask, 'why should you want to speak up for them?'

'I'm not s-s-speaking up for them,' whispers Yevgraf Ivanovich in an even more hushed voice, 'but can't you see who's sitting two paces away behind your back?'

'Who's sitting behind my back? How should I know? I haven't got eyes in the back of my head.'

Thereupon I turned round and looked: at the table behind me sat this great lump of a man in the uniform jacket of the victualling service, the very image, as Gogol put it, of 'a pig in a skull-cap'.* There he sits, the swine, stacking huge amounts of money on the cards, in the sort of nonchalant manner that was guaranteed to outrage downtrodden beggars like me: it was as if he were saying: 'Win or lose, I don't care. I do this strictly for the fun of it, because my granary is full. Eat, drink and be merry, that's my motto!' In a word, it was enough to make any poor beggar's gorge rise!

'Well, how do you like that?' I said. 'A prize specimen, and no mistake! How didn't I notice him before?' And, do you know, seeing the enemy at close range like that, I don't know what devil got into me, and instead of keeping my mouth shut, I started off on the same tack, even louder than before, and, what's more, laying it on as thick as I knew how.

'Brigands!' I say, 'leeches, that's what they are, these greedy-guts of commissaries! While the blood of us poor officers and soldiers was, as you might say, dripping into the Crimean dirt like beetroot kvass through a leaky bung, what were they doing? Robbing us, they were, lining their rascally pockets, building themselves houses and buying themselves country estates!'

Yevgraf Ivanovich nearly choked as he whispered:

'G-G-Give it a rest!'

But I go on:

'Why should I? Isn't it the truth that we were perishing of hunger: that thanks to their good offices what we got for grub was mouldy salt beef and cabbage; that we bound our wounds with straw instead of lint, while they were swigging their sherry and dry madeira?'

I really went to town at their expense, I can tell you. The chaps I'd been talking to, seeing that I was getting up a good head of steam, let me get on with it, though now and again the ones who'd had a drop more to drink would laugh and start tapping their sherry glasses with their fingernails. As for dear old Yevgraf Ivanovich, poor timid chap, he was absolutely covered in confusion on my behalf: he picked up a handful of deuces from the table, spread them with both hands into a fan and hid his face behind them, whispering:

'Ooh, Porfiry Nikitich, ooh, the sh-sh-shameless fellow, what is he going on about? Have a bit of m-m-mercy . . .'

This coyness of his made me even more furious.

'That's just the way it always is with us Russians,' I thought, 'the man who's right, the one with a clean conscience, sits and blushes, while the double-dyed rogue, just like Vaska, the cat who's stolen the cream,* stuffs his belly with what he's pinched and doesn't twitch a whisker.'

And with that I took a look behind me at the table where the commissary who had irritated me so much was sitting, and I could see that indeed he hadn't twitched a whisker. It just wasn't possible that he hadn't heard all my pronouncements to the world at large about his esteemed fraternity: yet he was sitting quite unmoved, smoking a large fragrant cigar and playing a trump. And since everything about a man depends a good deal on the mood he's in, it seemed to me that he played his trump, or, for that matter, all his cards, in a somehow similarly revolting manner. You know what I mean – it was as though he tossed them down without so much as a flick of the fingers, as if to say: 'There, you scum, take that, and see if I care.' I hated him all the more because he had, you might say, scored a point off me by remaining so unruffled. There's me, splitting my seams, hurling abuse, snapping at him like a mongrel at an elephant, and he doesn't even bat an eyelid. So I come on even stronger.

'You're having us on,' I thought to myself, 'and may the wolves devour you! I'll stir you into action, you see if I don't. I, my lad, am a Russian and I shan't stand on ceremony. Whether my host likes it or not, I'm going to hit you where it hurts.' And hit him I did. I let fly everything I knew about him personally, in light allegorical disguise.

'We decent Russian folk,' I said, 'whom nobody would dare accuse of thieving, we, who were wounded and maimed in the war, still can't get a job for ourselves anywhere; we haven't even got enough to feed our wives. But these arch-swindlers, once they've made a name for themselves as first-rate locusts, they never look back; they've got a job in the service even in peacetime, their wives go around in silk and velvet, and their floozies are even better turned out . . .'

On I went, ranting and raving, till I finally gave up, exhausted . . . I was running out of words and my throat was getting sore, but still he didn't turn a hair. The fact was, he was holding all the trumps: even Yevgraf Ivanovich noticed as much, and started chaffing me:

'W-W-Well,' he whispers, 'well, old f-f-fellow, and where's all your eff-ff-ffrontery got you, eh?'

'You keep your "old f-f-fellow" to yourself,' I answered, 'and sit quiet.'

But to be honest, you know, I really did feel crushed. What's more, all I'd seen so far was the blossom; the berries were still to come.

Shortly before supper the card game broke up; the players started settling their accounts. Our victualler had won a fortune; he pulled from his pocket a monstrous great wallet stuffed with hundred-rouble notes and added his winnings to them – another twenty or so of the same. He then tucked the whole lot back in his pocket with the same unperturbed, but very perturbing, nonchalance.

Well, at this point everyone got to their feet and took a stroll to stretch their legs. Just then our host came up to our table and said:

'So, my good fellows, what have you been up to? Loafing about and scandal-mongering, it would appear.'

'Could you hear us too?' I said.

'I should think I could,' he says. 'Your worship was bawling as though he were on the deck of a ship.'

'Stepan Aleksandrovich,' I said, 'I beg you, please forgive me.'

'What do I have to forgive you for? It's God that'll forgive you.'

'I lost my temper,' I said, 'I just couldn't restrain myself.'

'And why should you have?'

'When I saw him,' I said, 'I just boiled up inside, and even though I felt that I was putting you in an awkward position . . .'

'What on earth did you do that affects me?'

'Well he *is* your guest . . .'

'Oh that . . . Listen, old man, that's nothing to me. All sorts of types turn up here. I've set up the ark, and all sorts of creatures come in two by two: the riff-raff come in dozens. This Anempodist Petrovich, by the way, is a very clever type; he won't take umbrage at trifles like that.'

'He won't?' I asked in surprise.

'Of course he won't.'

'You mean he's so thick-skinned?'

'Thick-skinned? Good heavens, no. On the contrary, he's a sensitive man; but he's canny, and takes a broad view of things. What's more, he's no raw apprentice in these matters; he's taken a beating or two in his time, I don't doubt. As for your rude names, people call his type rude names wherever they go.'

'And yet they still do go everywhere – to people's houses?'

'Why shouldn't they, if people let them in, or even invite them?'

Host or no host, that angered me.

'That's just the problem with us, your honour,' I say. 'We curse worthless types like that, then welcome them into our homes. Griboyedov commented upon that fact in his time,* and nothing has changed since.'

'Nor will it, because there's no other way it can be.'

'Don't go on,' I said, genuinely dismayed. 'Why is it, for instance, that in England . . .' (At that time, owing to the influence of Katkov's journal *The Russian Messenger*,* England was all the rage.)

But I had hardly got the word 'England' out before Stepan Aleksandrovich measured me with his sombre eye and interrupted: 'What are you trying to do, foist Katkov's mumbo-jumbo on us? It's no good our trying to ape the English.'

'Why not? Are you trying to say the English are angels, not ordinary people like us?'

'Oh, they're people all right; it's just that they have different ways.'

'I'm not talking about politics,' I said.

'Nor am I. We, thank God, are Russian gentry, not English lords; we don't have to stuff our noble heads full of politics. That there are perhaps more honest or, at least, decent folk in England than here in Russia – that's the truth as you see it. But then what's so surprising about that? In England it makes sense to be an honest man, whereas there's no profit in being a rogue: in those circumstances, the honest have bred and multiplied. Over there, everyone is brought up that way from earliest childhood, told to "be a gentleman"; and they explain to the child what that means. But we instil a different maxim: "Righteous men do not live in fine houses." Now a child is no fool: he knows which side his bread is buttered on. So he follows the path that he has been shown. You've got to look at all this in a sensible way, from the point of view of personal advantage, and not like you sailors do, with your silly idealism. That's why you're such a useless lot.'

'What do you mean by that?' I said.

'Exactly what I say: you're about as useful as a fifth leg on a donkey. Let's imagine, for instance, that you're looking for a job and I put in a good word for you along the following lines: "This chap is an officer in the Black Sea Fleet, as honest as the day is long, never puts his hand in the till or lets anyone else do the same, and will go to the wall in the cause of justice." Well, I won't get you the job, and I won't do myself any good either. They'll call me a fool for taking your part. They'll say: "He's a fine enough fellow, that friend of yours, but we don't need a man like that, we need someone who's not quite so perfect." So the fact is, I shan't go and put in a word for you, whereas for him, for that fine gentleman over there (our host nodded in the direction of the commissary, who was standing at the buffet table) I'd put my oar in anywhere, because in our sort of society types like that are always in demand, and guarantee success to whoever takes them on.'

'Are you trying to tell me,' I said, 'that that's how it has to be?'

'Yes, of course. You see, he's a very smart, adaptable sort of fellow; anyone can see how best to make use of him; whereas you —what good are you to anyone? With your fine sense of truth and justice, you'll just squabble with everybody. The only thing to do with your sort is pick them up by the tail and toss them back on to a ship, because here on shore you'll just sit and gather dust.'

Well now, take note, gentlemen, – said Porfiry Nikitich emphatically, – I'm not spinning a yarn. This is no tale made up to amuse you. I'm reporting the actual words of a real person, which must have some historical significance, if not in history textbooks, then at least in the oral traditions of our seafaring brotherhood. That's how people saw us in those days, gentlemen – not just as men of honour among ourselves, but as impeccably moral types in general. But that's all beside the point. Let me tell you more of what happened over supper at Khrulyov's.

'So you see, my good honest fellow,' said Stepan Aleksandrovich in conclusion, giving me a friendly slap on the back, 'the age of ideals is past. Nowadays even a man who doesn't know a word of Latin will tell you "suum cuique" – "to each his own". Why don't we go and have a bite to eat instead, or else your Anempodist Petrovich, regular pig that he is, will as likely as not scoff all the salmon single-handed – which would be a pity, for it's a good one. I got it as a sample from Smurov's on Morskaya Street. Incidentally, while we're eating, I'll introduce you to him.'

'Introduce me? To whom?'

'To Anempodist Petrovich.'

'No, thanks very much.'

'What? You mean you'd rather not?'

'Absolutely.'

'A shame: he's a very shrewd man – statesmanlike, you might almost say – and yet at the same time he's a Russian through and through. He's a man who sees to the very heart of things, a man who'll go far.'

'Well, good luck to him, that's what I say.'

'Yes, quite. But you know, he's an amiable fellow and one you could learn a good deal from.'

'Good grief!' I thought. 'What virtues will he find in him next! The sort you can learn from, indeed! Pah!'

We went over to the buffet and mingled with the throng. Anempodist Petrovich, who had established himself at its centre, was delivering an edifying address. I concentrated on trying to catch a few of the prophecies emanating from this oracle.

The only thing he talked about at first, however, was the salmon. His comments were indeed substantial and founded on a considerable expertise. All of which seemed to me quite enough to make any decent man sick.

He sucked and chewed and smacked his lips, voluptuously testing each morsel on his tongue and palate; this procedure ensured a more precise sampling, a finer evaluation of the salmon. He delicately savoured it, then, just like Gogol's Petukh,* pronounced through closed lips:

'Mm . . . mm . . . yes . . . not bad . . . not at all bad . . . in fact, pretty good . . . you might say.'

'Very good salmon indeed,' someone remarked.

'Mm . . . mm . . . yes . . . possibly . . . mm . . . pretty fair . . . it *is* tender . . .'

'Why, it's as soft as butter.'

'Mm . . . mm . . . yes . . . you could say it has . . . mm . . . a certain buttery quality . . .'

'Well, I must say, you're sparing in your praise.' This intervention came from a colonel with a scar running the width of his forehead and across the bridge of his nose. 'After the muck we got in the Crimea, anything seems good. You couldn't get hold of stuff like this down there.'

'Mm . . . mm . . . well . . . is that really so? . . . We . . . mm . . . managed to get it all right, even there.'

'But at a price, I'll warrant.'

'Mm . . . true, yes, of course, one had to pay . . . but we got plenty of it . . . for ourselves . . . through Kiev . . . we ordered it from the merchant Pokrovsky . . . good salmon it was, too . . . they actually called it "commissariat salmon". Yes . . . this Pokrovsky, incidentally, also supplied salmon for the royal table – only that, of course, wasn't quite the same quality; you see, they didn't dare charge His Majesty what they charged us. But we . . . it didn't matter to us – we had the money.'

The colonel with the scar heaved a sigh.

'You certainly weren't short of money,' he said, 'in fact you had so much you didn't know what to do with it.'

'That's perfectly true; indeed, some of our chaps were not used to it and didn't know where to stop . . . mm . . . one of them, I remember, heard about "jeroboam pockets", and ordered his tailor to make him some. Well, it was a farce; the tailor thought it must mean some sort of fine material, and so made the pockets out of damask. That really caused some amusement.'

'What *did* it mean then?'

'Well, big enough to hold a jeroboam of wine . . . mm . . . mm . . . you see, our wallets were . . . mm . . . so fat . . .'

'Why, you unholy swine!' I thought. 'And he hasn't even the decency to keep his mouth shut!'

Meanwhile he was going on with a tale about some fellow of theirs in victualling or the commissariat, who at that terrible time, in the midst of universal suffering and the hardships of war, went even more berserk.

'This chap,' says he, 'all of a sudden lost whatever sense of taste he ever had, and started guzzling God knows what crazy stuff.'

'Aha,' I thought, 'that's splendid. I wish the whole lot of you would do the same and poison yourselves.' But the 'crazy stuff' in question turned out to be something quite unexpected.

'This chap had always liked kvass,' Anempodist Petrovich went on, and kvass was his regular tipple. He came from a good solid background – he'd been educated at a seminary. His father was an archpriest and a well-known preacher; in his last testament he enjoined his son, if he had the means to buy wine, to drink beer; if he had the means to buy beer, to drink kvass; and if he had the means to buy kvass, to drink water. But in fact he touched nothing but kvass, and wanted nothing but kvass – but then during the campaign he began to add champagne to it . . .'

'How do you mean?'

'Just like I say . . . mm . . . he mixed them in equal portions: he'd pour half a glass of kvass and half a glass of champagne, stir and drink.'

'What a pig!' I muttered, but so indiscreetly that Anempodist Petrovich heard me and, casting a glance in my direction, observed:

'Yes, pretty loutish behaviour, I grant you. Mind you, I should just say that champagne and kvass is not such a bad mixture as you might think . . . Indeed, during the war, it became quite a fashion among our chaps in the victualling service . . . mm . . . quite a few of the lads still drink it . . . they've acquired the taste. Now foreigners, they can't drink it . . . we did try giving them some just for the fun of it . . . and they . . . er . . . spat it out . . . just didn't have the stomach for it.'

Now I may not be a foreigner, but I myself felt like spitting and leaving – when suddenly this splendid specimen of an Anempodist Petrovich turns to me in the most casual fashion and says:

'By the way, forgive me, I beg you, but, if you'll allow me, I'd like to raise one tiny objection to what you were saying about the Russian character.'

I really can't say why, but instead of cutting him dead with some insult or other, I answered:

'Oh, do be so kind, tell me.'

'Well,' says he, 'in a nutshell, I'll say only this: what you had to say about us Russians was hurtful and unfair.'

That brought me to my feet, I can tell you.

'What! I? Hurtful!'

'Yes. While I was sitting playing cards, I kept picking up snatches of what you were saying to your comrades, and I rather took offence on behalf of all my compatriots. Believe me, you've really no right to defame the Russian nation in that way.'

'Who – I?' I said. 'You say *I* defame the Russian nation?'

'Why yes, of course you do. What was it you were saying? . . . I listened to you for some time . . . you divided the Russian people into two halves, your suggestion being that one half consisted of entirely honourable folk, heroes as it were, while the other half were nothing but thieves and scoundrels.'

'Aha!' I said, 'so that's what you find hurtful, is it?'

'No, sir. Absolutely nothing offends me personally, because I also inherited a precept from my father, a nobleman – namely, that one should never take anything unpleasant that one hears as referring to oneself. But I do take offence on behalf of all other Russians at your unwarranted slur. I believe that we Russians are all, without exception, capable of every possible human virtue. You stated, sir, that when you – that is to say, fighting soldiers – were shedding your blood in the mud of the Crimea, at that same time we in the victualling service were robbing and stealing – and that is perfectly true.'

'Yes,' I replied heatedly, 'I can assure you it is true. And now, having heard your disgraceful story about the kvass and the champagne, I'm even more convinced that I was right to say what I did.'

'Well, let's leave aside the kvass and the champagne: that's just a matter of taste – some like one thing, some like another. King Friedrich added asafoetida to his food, but I don't see anything particularly disgraceful even in that. But as concerns your division of us Russians into two widely differing categories – with that I cannot agree. The way I see it, you know, one shouldn't go giving a bad name to no less than half a nation. We're all created from the same rib and anointed with the same oil.'

'Now wait a minute,' I said. 'All anointed with the same oil we may be, but that doesn't mean we're all thieves.'

He tried to give the impression he hadn't quite caught what I had said, and asked:

'What was that?'

I repeated, straight to his face:

'*We* are not thieves.'

'That I know, sir. How could you be expected to be thieves? Why, you haven't had the chance yet to learn the art of stealing. The late Admiral Lazarev instilled in you a sense of honesty, to which, for the time being anyway, you still cling. But what lies in the future – that God alone knows . . .'

'No, that will never change!'

'And why not?'

'Because those who serve with me are honourable men.'

'Honourable men! For goodness' sake, I'm not disputing that. They are very honourable men, but that's no reason to assert that only your chaps are honourable, whereas others are dishonourable. Fiddlesticks! I insist on speaking out in their defence, and in defence of all Russians, for that matter! Yes, sir! Take my word for it, you are not the only ones who can quietly suffer hunger, fight, and die like heroes; but to hear you talk, the only thing we have been capable of doing, since the day we were baptised, is thieving. Fiddlesticks, sir! Not true, sir! We Russians – it's the fate of every one of us, it's part of that breadth of character with which we are all endowed – we have the capacity for anything. We're like cats: throw us where you will, we'll never land face-down in the dirt; no, we'll land foursquare on our feet; whatever fits the bill, we'll show we've got it in full measure: if it's a question of dying, we'll die, if it's stealing, we'll steal. You were asked to fight, and you did it as well as it could be done – you fought and died like heroes and earned fame throughout Europe for it. But we found ourselves in a business where a man could steal: and we too made a name for ourselves; we thieved so well that our fame also spread far and wide. But if, let's say, an order had come through for us all to swap places, with us ending up in the trenches and you in army supply, then we thieves would have fought and died, and you . . . would have thieved . . .'

That's what he said, as bold as brass!

I was just on the point of snapping back: 'Why, you dirty dog!' But everybody else was absolutely delighted by the man's candour, and they started shouting:

'Bravo, bravo, Anempodist Petrovich! Shameless – but how neatly put!' And they all burst into jolly laughter, as though he'd just told them some marvellous good news or other about themselves. Even Yevgraf Ivanovich couldn't restrain himself and stuttered:

'It's the t-t-truth!'

Meanwhile, he, the thick-skinned devil, had stuffed his mouth full of salmon again, and started reading me another homily.

'Of course,' he says, 'if all that rubbish you were talking earlier can be put down to your inexperience, then God will forgive you: but in future, just you watch what you have to say about your own people. Why praise some and find fault with others? We are all, every single one of us, capable of absolutely everything, and, God willing, by the time you die, you will have come to see that for yourself.'

So that's the way it ended. I was left the guilty party, and got a ticking off into the bargain from this paragon of practical wisdom, to the approval of all present. Well, as you will appreciate, after that little lesson, I pulled my horns in a bit and . . . to be perfectly honest, nowadays I quite often recall the brazen cheek of the man, and I get to thinking that, for all I know, the shameless rascal may have been right.

The Robber

We were on our way to Makary's fair.* Our conveyance was a huge tarantass* of Tambov manufacture. Inside sat five passengers: myself, a merchant from Nizhny Lomov, the agent for an Astrakhan trading company, and two juniors who were travelling with him. The merchant, the agent and I were sitting at the rear, under the hood; the juniors sat facing us. A sixth passenger, a peasant trader from the village of Golovinshchina, was riding up on the box beside the coachman. We had wanted to use post-horses, but were afraid of being delayed in the province of P**, where at that time the post-stations were under the control of General Tsyganov (I've made up the name). He held the office of Marshal of the Nobility, and spent more and more of his time hunting foxes and other noble quarry, while completely neglecting his administrative duties. Meanwhile, those beneath him, who could rely on his protection, did exactly as they pleased. A local fair provided them with rich pickings: there were travellers aplenty, for the most part merchants, men of means and not the sort to cause trouble: you could do what you pleased with them; they wouldn't cause a fuss or quibble over the odd rouble, since they would always reckon on recouping it. In any case, at Tsyganov's post-stations, nobody much cared even if there was trouble. 'Why should we worry about complaint-books?' they would say. 'We don't care a toss for your complaint-book.* For three roubles we can get a nice new one put on the table.' Knowing all this, we decided to use hired horses. While this mode of travel was likewise hardly the last word in comfort and convenience, it was still to be preferred, in that at least one could expect less downright unpleasantness. The weather was clear and dry, the ground beneath us as good as a metalled road, except for the clatter of the wheels. As is always the case, we quickly got to know each other, and established that sort of friendly intimacy of which only Russian travellers seem capable. There was never a break in the conversation; indeed, the merchant, who was constantly covering his face with a blue cotton handkerchief and settling down for a nap, got quite cross with us, and kept grumbling under his breath. Actually he was only annoyed when we were on the move; whenever we halted, he would immediately join in the conversation himself. The most loquacious of our company, whose constant chatter did become quite tiresome, was one of the juniors travelling with the agent from Astrakhan. His name was Gvozdikov. He was an extraordinarily jovial young fellow, with very pleasant features – you know, not particularly intelligent, but open, jolly; in a word, pleasant. Every second minute he would resume his chattering, teasing his companion with ever more wicked jibes. The look in his eyes was so innocent, his laughter so gentle, that this light-hearted jollity of his became almost too much to bear. The other junior, Gvozdikov's comrade, was a man of about forty, whose eyes were surrounded by a veritable thicket of black hair. This hair was cut in a fringe just above his eyes, giving him the typical appearance of a Russian sectarian. Actually, he freely admitted that he lived 'according to the old belief'.* He laughed at his comrade's sallies somewhat less than whole-heartedly, and was for ever trying to turn the conversation to such erudite topics as the Scriptures or some question of morality. Gvozdikov referred to him as 'the yellow-eyed seal'. The agent himself, a stout, sturdy man with a broad bushy beard, also trimmed in the Russian fashion, was not what you'd call a particularly imposing person; but he was a kind and indulgent man. The peasant sitting up by the driver remained silent for practically the whole journey, his only contribution being the occasional irrelevant query, which our jovial junior always hastened to answer with some smart quip.

We spent nearly an entire day in Arzamas, and left only as evening was drawing on. By the time we had covered fifteen versts, we were overtaken by the dusk, and the village where we were due to change horses was already wrapped in darkness. To the woman who came out on to the porch to meet us our first request was that she set up the samovar. Each of us wearily carried in some item of luggage – a travelling bag, a bundle, a string of cracknels.* We left the 'yellow-eyed seal' to guard the tarantass. When we entered the wooden house, the air was frightfully stuffy. We carried a table out into the passageway, drew up some benches, and laid out our provisions. An hour later the woman brought us the samovar: it was reddish-brown, stained with green, and had a dripping tap.

'Shall I harness up your horses?' she enquired, putting a wooden bowl beneath the dripping tap.

'Yes, you go ahead and harness them up, my precious beauty!' replied Gvozdikov.

'Where are all the menfolk, then? Or are you on your own here?' asked the merchant.

'On my own? Why should I be on my own? I'm not on my own. God is with me.'

'So God takes care of you, does he?'

'Who else? Of course he does.'

'And who are the menfolk round here?'

'Menfolk?'

'Yes.'

'Who? There's my father-in-law, my husband, and his young brother – but he's no more than a lad.'

'And you're the only woman?'

'I am. We buried my mother-in-law in the spring, and we shall be marrying the lad in the autumn.'

'And where have they all got to, the menfolk?'

'Oh! The lad set off driving early this morning; he's also taking merchants to the fair, and he isn't back yet. My husband and his father are not far away. They're over at our neighbour's, helping the local policeman with an enquiry.'

'What enquiry is that?'

'Well, it happened just the other day: a traveller had the luggage cut from the back of his carriage.'*

'Who did it?'

'Who can tell? There's all sorts up and down the road these days: it's the fair.'

'And when will they be back from seeing the policeman?'

The woman spat on two fingers and pinched the snuff from the candle.

'They should be back any minute now. They left at first light.'

We drank a cup of tea, then another. The gate into the yard creaked open, and we heard the sound of voices. A moment later a tall muzhik came into the passageway: his expression was not so much stern as vexed and angry. Without so much as a nod in our direction, he walked past us into the house.

'Is Mikitka still not back?' he asked the woman in a rather impatient, irritable tone.

'Not yet.'

'Why haven't you lit the lamp? Get things ready for supper.'

He reappeared in the doorway, and without a word of welcome, said:

'You'd do well to bring the tarantass into the yard.'

'Why so? We're travelling on.'

'A fine time you've chosen for travelling!' he muttered, and, turning to the woman, shouted: 'Get on with the supper, d'you hear! Or are you deaf or something?'

From the house we heard: 'There's no need to bawl your head off. I'm doing it, can't you see?'

The muzhik went out into the yard, and we again heard the sound of voices. A few minutes later the voice of an old man, right by the door into the passageway, said: 'I've given them fodder, can't you hear? I told you I'd done it. They're feeding.'

An old man entered, as white as a winter ptarmigan, and with a slight stoop.

'Enjoy your tea, honoured merchants!' he said.

'Come and join us, and welcome, old man!' the agent responded, but the old man, obviously considering this invitation to be merely a formality, paid no heed to it.

'So you want to move on, eh?' he asked, resting his elbows on our table.

'We do.'

'You're in a hurry, I suppose?'

'We are.'

'Going to the fair?'

'Yes.'

Pausing for thought, he said: 'It's not a good idea to go on now', and he looked each of us in turn in the eye.

'Why not?'

'There's still mischief afoot out there.'

'Mischief?'

'Yes. They're up to their tricks, damn them. Cossack sentries were posted a couple of days ago – they're manning a picket line down in the dell; but only yesterday our neighbour, a landowner, was taking his young son somewhere in his own carriage, and they cut the whole back of it to bits.'

'Who did?'

'God alone knows.'

'And nobody saw them?'

'Well the *barin* was sitting in the back with his wife, of course, but they felt nothing; and the lackey was dozing up on the box, I suppose. So who could have seen them?'

'What about the driver?'

'Well, maybe he saw nothing either.'

'And maybe he did?' queried Gvozdikov.

'Who can tell? Maybe he did. But what are you supposed to do with rogues like that?'

'What's the cause of it all?'

'It's the fair.' This answer, delivered in a similarly nervous tone, came from the husband of the woman who had met us. He had suddenly returned from outside, carrying a lantern and a bridle.

Nobody spoke. We all felt very uneasy. The husband, addressing nobody in particular, went on: 'They're all in some mad rush. You tell them – wait a bit, take your time, but it's a waste of breath, they don't want to listen. Then it's us poor sinners who keep getting dragged off to be questioned.'

'What do they do that for?' the agent enquired.

'You better ask them that question.'

'Well,' said the old man gently, 'they ask you whether you've seen anything, or whether you've heard anything.'

'Surely all you have to do is tell them, and then off you go.'

'It's not as simple as that.'

'They keep on plaguing you with questions, you see,' the old man added. 'They keep trying to get out of you what maybe you've never seen in the first place.'

'Well, you should just tell them.'

'Tell them what?' the younger man asked again.

'The truth.'

'The truth! Nowadays, my friend, the truth walks barefoot and with an empty belly.'

The woman brought out a large bowl of kvass, with something floating in it, and put it down next to us on the end of the table, together with three wooden spoons and a hunk of bread. The two muzhiks and the woman turned to the door, through which we could see a patch of dark sky, crossed themselves, and began to eat. The old man perched himself beside the merchant; the younger man and the woman ate standing up. Gvozdikov emptied his cup and went out to relieve the 'yellow-eyed seal'. The latter came in, sat down, poured a cup of tea, bit off a lump of sugar, and, crossing himself with two fingers,* began to sip his tea.

'It's not a good idea to move on now,' he said, finishing his first cup and reaching for the teapot.

'Why not?' we asked, practically in unison.

Our hosts went on with their supper and gave the appearance of taking no interest whatsoever in what we were saying.

'They say there's a good deal of mischief hereabouts during the night.'

'Well, there are five of us.'

'That would really frighten them, there being five of you!' interposed the younger peasant.

'You would make six.'

'What have I got to do with it? How can I see what's going on? My job is to keep my eyes on the road.'

'Where does the coachman come into it, your honour, sir?' said the old man. 'Sometimes, even what the coachman sees, he doesn't see.'

'How do you mean?'

'I mean just what I mean.'

'Why shouldn't he shout to warn his passengers?'

'Aye, but if I'm on my way back, then who do I shout to?' the younger man rejoined.

'Well, in those circumstances, what reason is there to shout?'

'The same reason.'

'Eh, good merchants, it can't be done,' the old man said. 'When we've delivered you to where you're going, we have to come back again – and he can be lying in wait for us somewhere, with a club in his hand, aye, and very likely not on his own either. He'll steal our animals, or even do us in as well.'

'Oh come, what nonsense!'

'Why should I be making it up? Haven't such things been known to happen?' the younger man again intervened.

'No, my friend, it's out of the question; there's absolutely nothing at all that we can do about them,' said the old man.

'A fine brave lot you are, I can see.'

'What's "brave" got to do with it? You can be as brave as you like, but you won't be braver than the *mir*,' the younger man again observed.

'What's the *mir* got to do with it?'

'The *mir*?'

'Yes.'

'Well, you're a clever one, aren't you? What's the *mir* got to do with it, you ask? What if, out of spite, the robber sets fire to my house and ends up burning the whole village down, eh? And you ask, what's the *mir* got to do with it?'

'Oh, I see, now he's likely to burn the whole village down, is he?'

'What, do you think I'm telling you fairy-tales?'

'What about the Cossacks?'

'Well, what about them? They're only any good at what they're good at – stealing our chickens and chasing our women. Anyway, they may well be in cahoots.'

'With the robbers?'

The young muzhik did not reply.

Instead, the old man said: 'Who can tell? You hear all sorts of rumours, but we . . . God knows. Only the authorities know what sort of folk they've sent to protect us.'

'It looks like we're spending the night here, gentlemen,' said the agent to the rest of us.

'Oh well, if we must, we must,' we all said, more or less in chorus.

All desire to travel on had been knocked out of us. Our hosts betrayed no particular interest in our decision, apart from the younger man, who seemed to calm down, and after swallowing a mouthful or two of soup, said, in a tone we had not heard from him previously:

'It's no skin off his nose – the robber's, I mean – whether he does you in or burns down a whole village. He doesn't care; it's the only sort of life he knows. But if we go and interfere, what happens? We get dragged off and pestered – why didn't we stop them, why didn't we catch them? Then there's the *mir* – they hold you to blame for the whole wretched business.'

'Do you ever catch sight of these rogues?'

'What if we do?'

'Don't misunderstand me. I mean, is it possible to get a glimpse of them?'

'And why shouldn't you? A bear is a wild beast, yet you can catch a sight of him, so why shouldn't you be able to see a man?'

'And *have* you ever?'

The muzhik didn't reply immediately, and put down his spoon. The woman picked up his bowl and went to fetch his *kasha.**

'Six years ago or so, or maybe longer,' he said, 'I had such a fright as God forbid I ever have another like it.'

We all pricked up our ears in interest.

'About ten versts from here, just off the main road, there's a village; it's a big place, we'll pass it tomorrow, maybe. Anyway, one of the peasants there had a horse for sale. Our muzhiks kept going on about what a good gelding it was, in fine fettle and sound as a bell. Well, as it happened, our own horse had just gone lame, and it was the same time of year as now – the fair was on, there was lots of travelling to be done. So I got up early – well, I can tell you, it wasn't even daybreak – took about forty roubles with me, or maybe a bit more, and set off for the village. There I am, going through a wood, and I get to thinking: maybe I'll cut myself a cudgel; you never know what might happen, I think. So I look around in the bushes and spot a nice sturdy sapling with a good butt-end on it, you know the sort I mean. So I chop it down. I chop it down, and as I walk along, I trim off the side shoots with my knife, and the result is a really handy cudgel. Now, I think to myself, if I give anyone a wallop with this, it'll certainly give him something to think about – and I go on my way. Anyway, I carry on for another three versts or so, when suddenly, about thirty paces or so up ahead, sitting on the roadside right by the forest-edge, I spy a man. He's sitting with his legs dangling down into the ditch, no hat on his head, long hair - a bit like a young sacristan has - wearing a scruffy pair of trousers, but no shirt. On his knees he's got a pile of rags of some sort, and he's picking through them, obviously searching for lice. I looked behind me and to both sides - there wasn't another living soul to be seen. I took fright. I thought, if I turn back, he'll chase me; but I was scared to go forward as well. 'Ah well,' I think, 'let the Lord's will be done. What God doesn't abandon, the pig can't eat.' I uttered a prayer and went on. As I drew near, he shook out the rags - all holes they were - and I could see it was a soldier's shirt. I walked on, closer and closer, with an icy chill in my heart. As I draw level with him, he stands up. I can see he's got nothing in his hands.'

The woman brought in the bowl of *kasha* and put it on the table. The muzhik crossed himself again, and, after eating a few spoonfuls, resumed his tale:

'He's standing there, and I've come right up to him. I take a look at him: a pitiful sight he is, his shoes tied round with string, black nankeen trousers with piping down the seam, looking like they were about to fall to bits, no shirt at all, just those rags thrown over his shoulders - made of the sort of cloth soldiers wear, you know, with the collar torn off.'

'Go on.'

'"A wretched specimen you are," I thought. I felt really sorry for him. He must be a deserter, I thought: my middle brother is in the army too. Really sorry I felt. I go up to him: he looks around and says as quietly as can be: "Give me a morsel of bread," he says, "for the love of God. It's four days," he says, "since anything passed my lips." "Dear oh dear, my friend," I says, "if only I'd known, but I haven't a crumb of bread on me". "Then give me a couple of kopecks," he says. Well, I thought to myself, I don't mind a couple of kopecks, and I'd have given him more than that, but I was scared. My money was wrapped in a rag and tucked into my boot. If I started fishing about – he was in a bad way, who could know what he might do! The devil is strong, I thought, and will incline a man to mischief, even when he's in less trouble than this fellow. "Don't be angry, my dear chap," I said, "but I haven't even got a couple of kopecks on me." "That can't be true," says he, "take pity on a fellow Christian, give me some money." At this point I hesitated a bit, you know, and I was going to get my money out – I just didn't know what to do. But just then the devil, you might think, took hold of his tongue. "Hand over," he says, "or I'll call my pals." And with that he bends down and shoves his hand into the top of his boot. Well, you see, there's his back all exposed to me, flat as a board. The fear of death got into me; there was no time for thinking, I could see that, so I raised my cudgel and brought it whistling down along the back of his neck, you know, as hard as I could. He pitched straight over and lay with his arms spreadeagled. There he was, face down, a bit like a frog, you might say. It wasn't as though he uttered a cry or turned his head. He just made a rattle in his throat and gave a short sigh. I turned on my heels and set off hell for leather. I don't know how I made it back to our village. The terror I felt – well, I wouldn't have the Madonna wish it on a Tatar.'

We looked at our host's athletic build and exchanged glances.

'And when you went back . . . he'd gone?'

'Yes, he'd gone. He must have crawled off into the forest.'

'Maybe you did him in?'

'When? Afterwards?'

'No. When you hit him.'

'God knows. If anything like that happened, it's a sin on my soul. But that wasn't what I intended. I said as much to the village elders, and when I confessed to the priest. The elders told me to keep quiet for the time being, and the priest didn't bar me from communion. 'You,' he said, 'bear no blame.' Still, he did impose penance. Mind you, they never did find a body any-where; I worried for a year or two, I thought he might turn up to prove my guilt; but no, he just vanished. Now, thank God, I don't worry any more.'

'What could have happened to him?' our peasant trader asked.

'Who can tell? Maybe he really did have some pals – they must have dragged him away,' the old man answered.

They had finished their supper, and we had emptied the teapot.

'Come on, let's go and bring in the tarantass,' the young peasant said to his father, and they left the room.

'Where will you sleep?' the woman said. 'In the house or outside?'

'Where is there to sleep outside?'

'Well, our travellers usually sleep in the barn, on the hay.'

'Aha! Well, that suits us.'

We went outside. The sky was starlit, the night was warm. A cow was loose in the yard: in the corner we could hear the snuffling of a horse. The peasants trundled in the tarantass and locked the gates.

'Going to sleep on the hay, good merchants?' our young host asked.

'That's right.'

'This way then.' He opened a small door into a tiny wattle-work barn, piled full of sweet-smelling hay.

'Here's a fine place for you to rest. Climb in. Is there anything I can bring you from your carriage? By the way, you'll be safe out here,' he added. 'You'll have nothing stolen. I sleep here myself.' He pointed to a high sleeping-platform set up on posts by the wall of the barn, right next to the gate.

We took with us only our pillows and a rug.

Five minutes later all that could be heard in the barn was the sound of snoring and whistling through the nose. You might have thought a quartet had struck up a tune. The merchant opened with a solo on the bass fiddle. Gvozdikov christened him 'the wooden tub', but promptly proceeded to improvise a few cadenzas himself. Not that it mattered much. Drowsy from the journey, everyone was sound asleep: I alone kept seeing in my dreams the young soldier of the previous evening's tale. I saw him crawling towards the forest, his face a deathly green, his eyes bulging, his lips blue, his tongue clenched between his teeth, and blood seeping from his eyes and nose. His tongue was also bleeding; while tucked behind the top of his boot were a little knife set in a home-made handle, wound round with old wire, a little Kievan cross of cypress wood, and a pinch of soil wrapped in a scrap of cloth. He must have carried that soil with him many a long mile, from his home village, where his aged mother and father still await their son's coming home on leave: and maybe a young wife is also waiting for him, or maybe she's hanging around with the Cossacks – or sitting with the old midwife, near her time.

Keep waiting, my friends, keep waiting.

An Iron Will

I

We were engaged in a furious argument: its fundamental premise was that the Germans are endowed with an iron will, which we Russians lack. For that reason, it was argued, easy-going types like us should avoid tangling with Germans, since we could hardly expect to get the better of them. Our topic, in other words, was absolutely commonplace, and yet, it must be said, as obsessive as it was tedious.

The only one of our company who refused to get involved was old Fyodor Afanasevich Vochnyov: instead, he calmly concentrated on pouring out the tea. When that was done, and we had each taken a glass, Vochnyov said:

'Gentlemen, I've listened carefully to what you've been saying, and it sounds to me like nothing but a lot of hot air. I mean, all right, let's assume that strength of will is a characteristic of our good friends the Germans, whereas we are a bit short of that particular commodity. Though that may be true, why should we be dismayed? No reason at all, as I see it.'

'How do you mean, no reason – when both we and the Germans have the feeling that's there's bound to be a conflict between us?'

'And what if there is?'

'They'll make a meal of us.'

'Oh come!'

'Of course they will, make an absolute meal of us.'

'Now steady on, I beg you: making a meal of us is not as simple as all that, you know.'

'What makes you think so? You're not putting any faith in alliances, are you? Hopes and dreams, my dear fellow, that's all the allies we shall have.'

'That may indeed be so – but then, why dismiss hopes and dreams so lightly? With respect, sir, you should know better. In the first place, hopes and dreams are good, warm-hearted Russian lads, ready to hurl themselves into fire and water when the occasion demands, and in our pragmatic times, that's worth a good deal.'

'Maybe so, but not when you're dealing with the Germans.'

'I disagree, sir. They are valuable precisely when dealing with the German, who will never take an unconsidered step, and, as they say, won't fall out of bed without calculating his trajectory in advance. In any case, aren't you attaching rather too much importance to will-power and calculation? In this connection one is bound to recall the somewhat cynical yet perfectly reasonable comment of a certain Russian general, who said of the Germans: I see no problem in the fact that they calculate everything so cleverly, because we shall present them with acts of such astonishing stupidity as will defy any effort they might make to understand them. And to be sure, gentlemen, that does surely give us some ground for hope.'

'What does, stupidity?'

'Yes, call it stupidity if you like: or, if you prefer, call it the brashness of a young, lively nation.'

'Oh, come on, old man, we've heard all that before. We're bored to death with that old fairy-tale about liveliness and youth – it has been told for a thousand years already.'

'So what if it has? I'm fed up to the teeth as well with all this talk of German iron: first it's the Iron Chancellor, then it's their iron will, then it's how they're going to eat us for their breakfast. Damn it all, I hope we give them a good belly-ache! Come, gentlemen, have your wits entirely deserted you? Maybe they *are* iron, while we are just plain, soft, raw dough – but you would do well to remember that dough, if there's enough of it, can't be chopped through even with an axe: what's more, an axe can get buried and lost.'

'Aha, so now you're back to the tired old notion that we can beat anybody with our eyes shut, are you?'

'No, nothing of the kind. I attach as little importance to that kind of idle boasting as I do to your empty fears. I refer only to the very nature of things, to what I have seen happen and to what I know happens when German iron encounters Russian dough.'

'Some minor incident, I suppose, from which you have drawn broad general principles?'

'Yes, an incident, and generalizations: but I have to say I cannot understand why you are against inferring general principles from single incidents. As I see it, there's no more to be said for your point of view than for that of the Englishman who, having listened to a résumé of Gogol's *Dead Souls*, exclaimed: "This nation is invincible." "Why?" he was asked. Astonished by the query, he replied: "How could anyone hope to conquer a people capable of producing such a scoundrel as Chichikov?"'

We couldn't help but laugh, and commented to Vochnyov that, whatever he might say, it was a funny way he had of praising his compatriots: at which he again scowled and replied:

'Forgive me, but you've all become so dogmatic and narrow-minded that an ordinary man of flesh and blood finds it very hard to talk to you. I tell you something simple and straightforward, and you all leap in to find some far-reaching conclusion or philosophical tendency. It's about time you began to break yourselves of this disgusting habit, and learned to take things as they come: I'm not praising my fellow-countrymen, and I'm not denouncing them either; I'm merely saying that they can look after themselves, and whether by dint of intelligence or stupidity, they'll give a good account of themselves. Should you find it interesting or hard to believe how such things can happen, then I can, if you like, tell you a tale about an iron will.'

'Won't the tale be rather long, Fyodor Afanasevich?'

'By no means. It's a short tale, which can be started and ended over tea.'

'Well, if it's short, go ahead: we can stand a short story, even about a German.'

'Then sit quietly, and I'll begin.'

II

Shortly after the war in the Crimea (it's not my fault, gentlemen, that all our stories these days seem to date from that period) I fell victim to a heresy fashionable at the time, and for which I have had ample cause to reproach myself since, that is, I abandoned my career in government service, after a fairly successful beginning, and took a job in one of the trading companies which were just re-establishing themselves at that time. The company in question has long since gone bankrupt and disappeared without trace. By working outside the public service I hoped not only to make an 'honest' living, but also to liberate myself from the whims of my superiors and from those unexpected turns of events which hang over every public servant, that is, the statute under which he may be summarily dismissed. I fancied, in a word, that I had become a free man, as though freedom begins just beyond the gates of a government office building: but that's all beside the point.

The company in which I found work was run by Englishmen: there were two of them, both married and with quite large families; one played the flute, the other the cello. They were both very kind and fairly practical men. This latter quality I deduced from the fact that, having once gone disastrously bankrupt, they realized that Russia has its peculiarities, which one ignores at one's peril. They then set up in business again, this time on simple Russian principles and once again – in perfectly English fashion – made themselves a fortune. However, at the time my story begins, they were still a bit lacking in experience, a bit 'green', as we say, and were squandering in the most idiotically self-confident manner the capital they had brought with them from home.

The firm was engaged in large and fairly complex operations: we ploughed land, sowed sugar-beet, and were setting ourselves up to refine sugar, distil spirits, saw timber, make barrel staves and parquet flooring, and manufacture saltpetre: in brief, we intended to exploit every commercial possibility the area had to offer. All these various projects we embarked on in one go, and the place was buzzing with activity: we were digging footings, building stone walls, erecting massive chimneys and taking on all sorts of people – though, mind you, they were, for preference, mostly foreigners. Among the highest-paid company staff I was the sole Russian – and that was only because among my other duties I was the company agent, for which position I was, needless to say, better fitted than my foreign colleagues. Still, there was a whole community of foreigners: the owners built small detached houses for us all, which, though somewhat uniform in appearance, were for all that very handsome and comfortable. They were grouped around the huge and ancient country mansion in which the owners themselves took up residence.

The mansion, which had been built with all kinds of architectural conceits, was so grand and capacious that two English households were able to settle in with ample space and every conceivable comfort. It was crowned by a semi-circular dome housing an Aeolian harp, which had, incidentally, long since lost all its strings: directly beneath this dome was a music room of massive proportions, where in times gone by serf musicians and singers had displayed their talents. These same performers had been sold off one by one by the previous owner as soon as rumours about the Emancipation had begun to seem something more than simply rumours. My English masters played Haydn quartets in this room: as an audience they invited all their employees, right down to foremen, office staff and ledger clerks.

This was all done in the name of 'cultivating good taste', though it can hardly be said to have succeeded, since these simple folk didn't much care for the classical quartets of Haydn: indeed, the music induced in them a profound melancholy. To me they complained in all frankness that 'there was no suffering worse than listening to that stinker', but listen to that 'stinker' they did, for all that – at least until fate bestowed upon us all a different and jollier form of amusement, in the form of the arrival from Germany of a new member of our colony, the engineer Hugo Karlovich Pectoralis. He came to us from the small town of Doberan* near the Plauersee in Mecklenburg-Schwerin, and the very mode of his arrival was itself fairly curious.

Since Hugo Pectoralis is destined to be the hero of my tale, I will give you a few details about him.

III

Pectoralis was consigned to Russia together with the machinery that he was to accompany, instal, put into operation and maintain. Why our English masters hired this German instead of one of their compatriots, and why they ordered the machinery from the little German town of Doberan, I cannot say for sure. It would appear that one of the Englishmen happened to see some machinery from this factory somewhere, took a fancy to it, and chose to turn a blind eye to certain patriotic conventions. A man's purse, after all, is not his brother, and even English patriotism has to pay it the respect which is its due. But look, do please stop me when I start wandering from the subject.

The machines in question were for our steam mill and timber yard: for both these enterprises the buildings had already been erected. We had been pressing hard for the despatch of both machines and engineer, and the manufacturer had informed us that the machines were on their way by sea to Petersburg with the latest batch of freight. As for the engineer – who we had requested should arrive in advance of the machines in order to prepare the buildings for their installation – we had received written word that the man would be sent off without delay, that his name was Hugo Pectoralis, that he was a master of his craft, and that he had the iron will to bring anything he did to a successful conclusion.

At that time I was on company business in Petersburg, so I got the job of taking delivery of the machines from the customs shed and sending them on to our own dark corner of the provinces: I was also entrusted with bringing back Hugo Pectoralis, who was due to arrive at any moment. I was to pick him up from the 'Sarepta House' of Asmus Simonsen and Co., better known to us as 'The Mustard House'. However, things went awry in the despatch both of the machines and of the engineer: the machines were delayed and finally arrived well behind schedule, whereas the engineer had exceeded all our expectations by arriving early in Petersburg. When I called in at 'The Mustard House' to leave an address at which I could be contacted by Pectoralis when he arrived, I was told that he had passed through already a week or so before.

This turn of events was a nuisance as far as I was concerned, but for Pectoralis constituted a considerable danger, occurring as it did at the end of October, which, as ill luck would have it, was that year marked by savagely inclement weather. The snow and frost had not yet set in, but torrential rains alternated with chilling mists: the northerly gales seemed intent on blowing the very marrow from one's bones, and the mire was everywhere so deep that one could imagine the diabolical state of the unmetalled post-roads. I could only assume that this – as it seemed to me – reckless foreigner, who had set out alone on such a long journey and at such a time, knowing nothing of our roads or our customs, must now be in a simply frightful situation. My assumptions were correct: indeed, reality exceeded my worst fears.

I had enquired at 'The Mustard House' whether the newly arrived Pectoralis had even a smattering of Russian, and was told that he had not. Not only did he not speak Russian; he did not understand a single word either. To my question whether he had sufficient money with him, I received the reply that he had been given travelling and subsistence allowances for ten days on the company's account, and had asked for nothing more.

The mess was getting worse. Bearing in mind the conditions of travel by post-chaise at that time, in conjunction with the inevitable interminable delays, one could imagine Pectoralis hopelessly stuck somewhere and, for all one knew, reduced to begging.

'Why didn't you stop him setting off? Couldn't you at least have persuaded him to wait for a travelling companion?' I asked reproachfully at 'The Mustard House'. To this they replied that they had tried to persuade him, and had made clear to him the difficulties he would face on the journey: but he had stubbornly insisted on doing things his own way. He had given his word, he said, to go straight to his destination without stopping, and he intended to keep that promise; moreover, he did not fear any difficulties that might arise, because he had an iron will.

In considerable alarm I wrote to my principals. I told them everything that had occurred and asked them to take all appropriate measures to counter the various misfortunes threatening our wretched wayfarer. Having written all this, however, I confess I had no clear idea myself how it might be done, how Pectoralis might be intercepted on the road and, in the care of a reliable companion, be delivered safely to his destination. It was quite impossible for me to leave Petersburg at that moment: I was

bound to await the arrival of some fairly important consign-
ments of goods. Moreover, Pectoralis had been gone so long that
I stood little chance of catching him up. If, on the other hand,
someone were despatched to meet this iron-willed specimen,
who could be sure that the envoy would cross paths with him
and recognize him?

At that time I was still under the illusion that anyone meeting
Pectoralis might fail to recognize him. This was a perfectly
natural consequence of the fact that the Germans whom I asked
about him were unable to describe to me any distinguishing
features of his. Precise and unimaginative as they were, they
gave me only the vaguest notion of the man – the sort of things
one puts on passports, and which could easily describe practically anyone at all. According to them, Pectoralis was a young
man of twenty-eight to thirty, slightly above average height,
slim, dark-haired, with grey eyes and a lively but resolute
countenance. I take it you'll agree that there wasn't much in that
to permit of instantaneous recognition. The most striking detail
which my memory retained from the entire description was the
'resolute and lively countenance', but what sort of ordinary chap
is so skilled in identifying the expressions on people's faces that
he could immediately have spotted him and uttered the chal-
lenge: 'Pectoralis, I presume'? What's more, who is to say that
the countenance itself might not have changed? The damp and
chill of a Russian autumn might well have rendered it considerably more flaccid and glum.

The upshot was then, that apart from the note I had written
on behalf of this weird fellow, there was really nothing more I
could do – and willy-nilly I took comfort in that fact. In any
case, just at that time I received orders out of the blue to make
several journeys to the south, which meant I had no time to
worry about Pectoralis anyway. October passed, and the first
half of November. Being constantly on the move, I heard no
news whatsoever of Pectoralis. I returned home only as Novem-

ber was drawing to its close, after a tour covering many towns and cities.

By this time the weather had changed appreciably: the rains had given way to bitter dry frosts, with daily dustings of powdery snow.

In the town of Vladimir I picked up a tarantass I had abandoned there: it stood me in good stead, since wheels still afforded easier travel than a sleigh. I promptly set off in it for home.

From Vladimir I had about a thousand versts to cover: I hoped to do it in six days or so, but the intolerable jolting and shaking so exhausted me that I allowed myself frequent breaks and thus made much slower progress. By the evening of the fifth day of my journey I had limped my way no further than Vasilev Maidan: at this spot a most unexpected and improbable encounter occurred.

I don't know how things are now, but at that time Vasilev Maidan was a cold, inhospitable post-station, stuck right out in the open. A fairly hideous building clad in weatherboarding, its porch adorned by a couple of dreary, lumpish columns, it looked out at the world with a hostile, unwelcoming stare. As far as I knew, the house was indeed a cold one: but I was so weary that I gritted my teeth and determined to stop the night.

A light flickering in the window of the travellers' room indicated the presence of other overnight guests: yet even that did not shake my determination to break my journey there. I was rewarded for my resolution by an extraordinarily pleasant surprise.

'You mean you met Pectoralis?' someone interrupted impatiently.

'Never mind who I met,' answered the storyteller, 'I would ask you to be patient, allow me to tell my story, and refrain from interrupting.'

'But what if I find your tale particularly interesting?'

'So much the better then: you can try to jot it all down and offer it as a *feuilleton* to one of our more interesting newspapers. The whole question of German will-power and our own lack of it is very much in vogue at the moment, and the tale I'm telling would make good copy.'

IV

I told my man to bring in my felt sleeping-bag, my fur coat and other necessaries, ordered the coachman to move the tarantass into the yard, and, having groped my way through a broad, dark passageway, began to fumble for the handle of the door. I eventually found it and started to tug, but the door had swollen tight in its frame, and wouldn't open. No matter how hard I pulled, my efforts alone would probably have proved inadequate to the task. Fortunately, however, someone's kindly hand – or rather, kindly foot – came to my assistance, for the door was suddenly kicked open from inside. I leapt backwards, and saw framed in the doorway before me a man in the standard top-hat of the city-dweller and an oilskin cape of exceedingly generous size, from the collar of which, tied by a string to one of the buttons, hung a large umbrella.

For a moment or two I was unable to make out the stranger's face, and I was, I confess, on the point of cursing him roundly for nearly having knocked me off my feet. However, what surprised me about him and particularly drew my attention to him was the fact that, instead of stepping through the door he had just opened, as one might have expected him to do, he on the contrary turned about and proceeded calmly to pace up and down the room. It was a bare, filthy room, dimly lit by a guttering tallow candle.

I asked him whether he knew where I could locate the station-master, or any other living soul for that matter.

'Ich verstehe gar nicht russisch,' the stranger replied.

I switched to German.

He was clearly delighted to hear the sound of his mother tongue and answered that the station-master wasn't about; he'd gone out some time ago.

'And you, I suppose, are waiting for horses?'

'Oh yes, I'm waiting for horses.'

'And aren't there any?'

'I'm not sure; but certainly none are given to me.'

'Have you asked?'

'No. I can't speak Russian.'

'Not a word?'

'Yes: "possible" . . . "impossible" . . . "customs" . . . "travel-warrant".'

These words, mouthed with some difficulty, apparently constituted his entire vocabulary.

'When they say "possible", I go. When they say "impossible", I don't go. If they say "travel-warrant", I hand it over, and that's about all.'

'Good grief,' I thought, 'what a specimen!'; and I took a closer look at him. What an outfit! His boots were perfectly ordinary, but from their tops emerged amazingly long red woollen stockings, which stretched above his knees and were supported half way up his thighs by blue ladies' garters. From beneath his waistcoat there hung down to his middle a knitted jersey of red worsted yarn. Over his waistcoat he sported a grey jacket made from the thick cloth normally reserved for dressing-gowns, with green edging; and on top of that was his totally unseasonable oilskin cape with the umbrella suspended from a button at the neck.

His entire luggage consisted of one tiny cylindrical bundle in an oilskin cover, which was lying on a table, a rather plain notebook, which was lying on top of the bundle, and nothing more.

'This is amazing!' I exclaimed, and nearly blurted out: 'Surely you're not travelling in that state, are you?' Fortunately, I just managed to avoid this gaffe, and turning to the station-master, who had just come into the room, ordered that a samovar be set up and the fire be lit.

My foreign friend was still pacing up and down; but when he saw the firewood being brought in and the fire being lit, he was suddenly transported with delight, and said:

'Aha, so it is "possible"; and I've been here three days already, and for three days I've been pointing at the hearth, and I've been told "not possible".'

'What? You've been here three days?'

'Yes, three days,' he replied calmly. 'Why do you ask?'

'Why on earth have you been sitting here for three days?'

'I've no idea. I wait like that everywhere.'

'At every station?'

'Oh yes, at every station, without fail. Ever since I left Moscow, I've waited everywhere, then gone on a bit.'

'And you have sat for three days at every station?'

'Yes, three days . . . that is, forgive me . . . at one I stayed two days, I made a note of it; but then on another occasion it was four days; I made a note of that too.'

'And what do you do while waiting at the post-stations?'

'Nothing.'

'Forgive me, I thought perhaps you were studying the local customs, or writing travel notes?'

That sort of thing was very much in vogue at the time.
'Well yes, I do observe the way I am treated.'

'Then why do you allow them to go on treating you like that?'

'Well . . . what can I do?' he replied. 'You see, I don't speak any Russian, and I am therefore obliged to defer to everyone. I had always accepted that that would be so; but later, you will see . . .'

'How do you mean, later? What will happen?'

'Later, I shall be the one in charge.'

'Oh, I see!'

'Oh, but I shall! There's no question about it!'

'Listen, how could you set off on such a journey, not knowing the language?'

'Quite simply, there was no option: our contract stipulated that I would travel without stopping on the way, and that's what I am doing. I'm the sort of man who always fulfils his promises to the letter,' the stranger replied, and, as he said it, his face, about which I had thus far come to no firm conclusions, suddenly assumed a 'lively and resolute' expression.

'My God, what a freak!' I thought to myself. 'Please forgive me,' I said, 'but can travelling the way you are travelling really be called "travelling without stopping on the way"?'

'What do you mean? I'm travelling all the time; as soon as they tell me "possible", I set off straight away; and in order not to waste time, I don't even take off my travelling clothes, as you can see. It's a very, very long time since I changed my clothes, I can tell you.'

'My dear fellow, you must smell as fresh as mint,' I thought to myself. I said:

'Pardon my asking, but I'm rather surprised at the way you arranged your journey.'

'In what sense?'

'Well, you'd have done better to seek out a Russian travelling companion in Moscow: that way you would have enjoyed a quicker and less troublesome journey.'

'But I should have had to spend time doing that.'

'Yes, but you would have made up the lost time very quickly.'

'I had determined, and given my word, that I would not stop.'

'But, as you yourself admit, you have been stopping at every post-station.'

'True, but not of my own volition.'

'I grant you that: but how on earth do you put up with it, and why?'

'Oh, I can endure anything: I have an iron will.'

'Good God!' I exclaimed, 'so you have an iron will, do you?'

'Yes, I have an iron will: my father had an iron will, as did my grandfather, and I too have an iron will.'

'An iron will! You are, sir, I assume, from Doberan in Mecklenburg Province?'

He answered in surprise: 'Yes, I'm from Doberan.'

'And you are on your way to the factories at R.?'

'That is indeed my destination.'

'And your name is Hugo Pectoralis?'

'Yes, yes indeed! I am the engineer Hugo Pectoralis: but how do you come to know?'

I could hold out no longer. I leapt to my feet, embraced Pectoralis like a long-lost friend and drew him over to the samovar, where I treated him to a warming glass of punch, and told him that I had recognized him by his iron will.

'So that's it!' he exclaimed, almost beside himself with delight, and, raising both hands heavenwards, solemnly uttered: 'O mein Vater, o mein Grossvater! Do you hear this, and are you content with your son Hugo?'

'They should certainly be well content,' I answered, 'but do sit down and drink some warm tea. I imagine you must be chilled to the bone!'

'Yes, I have been freezing. It's cold here. Oh, how cold it is! I've noted it down in my book.'

'And you're not properly dressed for the conditions. Those clothes you have on won't keep you warm.'

'It's true, they don't keep me warm a bit; only my socks do, that's all. But I have an iron will, and you can see how useful it is to have an iron will.'

'No,' I said, 'I can't.'

'How do you mean, you can't see? My reputation has travelled before me; I have kept my word; and I am alive and can die with no loss of self-respect, with no sign of having weakened.'

'Permit me to enquire, to whom exactly did you give your
word?'

'To myself.'

'To yourself! Pray permit me to observe; that amounts almost
to obstinacy.'

'No, it's not obstinacy.'

'But promises are given according to need, and fulfilled according to circumstances.'

A look of half-contempt crossed the German's face, and he
answered that he saw no virtue in that sort of maxim; that
anything he had once told himself must be done, would be done;
and that only in that way could one develop a truly iron will.

'To be master of myself and thus to become the master of
others – that is what must be, what I want, and what I will
pursue.'

'Well, my lad', I thought to myself, 'it looks as though you've
come here to astound us – just watch out, in case it's you that gets
a shock.'

V

Pectoralis and I spent the night in the same room and got hardly a
wink of sleep between us. He, having been chilled to the bone,
huddled in an armchair by the fire and felt not the slightest wish
to abandon this cosy spot: but he was as itchy as a flea-ridden
poodle – with the result that the armchair was constantly shifting
and creaking and waking me up. Several times I tried to persuade
him to shift to the couch, but he stubbornly refused. Early in the
morning we arose, drank tea, and departed. As soon as we
reached a town, I despatched him with my man to the public
bath-house. I instructed my man to have him well scrubbed and
fitted out with clean underwear: thereafter we were able to
proceed without further halts or further scratching. I also liber-
ated Pectoralis from his oilskin cloak, and wrapped him instead in

my man's spare fur coat: this enabled him finally to get warm again, as a result of which he became inordinately animated and loquacious. In the course of his slow peregrination, it turned out, he had not only frozen but also starved, since his subsistence allowance had run out. In any case he had immediately sent off a portion of this money to his home town of Doberan, and for the rest of the time virtually his only means of sustenance had been his iron will. On the other hand he had managed to compile a considerable quantity of by no means unoriginal observations and notes. He never failed to notice those things which no one had yet tackled in Russia, yet which could be overcome by the mere application of skill, persistence and, above all, iron will.

I was thoroughly content with my catch – both for myself and the other members of our colony. I reckoned that by bringing into their midst this weird and wonderful fellow who was already cooking up schemes to revolutionize Russia by the application of his iron will, I was ensuring a steady source of entertainment for them.

How successful he was in these ambitions will emerge from my tale: for the time being let us take things in their proper order.

I should say from the start that this Pectoralis turned out to be a very good man for the job – no genius, of course, but an experienced, knowledgeable and skilful engineer. Thanks to his determination and persistence, the job he had come to do progressed splendidly, despite all sorts of unexpected hitches. Many pieces of the machinery he had come to instal turned out to have been manufactured very inaccurately and from poor quality material. There was no time to enter into correspondence about this and demand replacement parts, because the corn was waiting to be ground. So Pectoralis made many of the things himself. These parts were cast, at a pinch, in a piddling little foundry in own run by a thoroughly idle tradesman known as Safronych. Pectoralis then machined them himself on a lathe. I have to say that to get this whole business sorted out did indeed require an iron will. Pectoralis's services did not pass unnoticed and were rewarded by an increase in his salary, which now amounted to fifteen hundred roubles a year.

When I told him of this increase, he thanked me in a dignified way and immediately sat down at his desk and began working out some figures: then, fixing his eyes on the ceiling, he declared:

'That means, without altering any of the decisions I've taken, the period can be reduced by exactly one year and eleven months.'

'What are you working out?'

'I'm just totalling up . . . certain personal considerations.'

'Oh, forgive me for prying.'

'Not at all, not at all: it's just that I have certain expectations, which depend upon my accumulating a certain amount of capital.'

'And the increase in salary I've told you about shortens the waiting period, I suppose?'

'Your supposition is correct: it shortens it precisely by one year and eleven months. I must write immediately to Germany with the news. Tell me, when do they take the post to town?'

'It goes today.'

'Today? What a pity! I shan't have time to describe everything as I would have liked.'

'Come now, what nonsense!' I said. 'As if one needs that long to inform a partner or a contractor about a matter of business.'

'Contractor?' he repeated, and added with a smile: 'Oh, if only you knew what sort of a contractor this was!'

'How do you mean? He's some dusty stickler for detail, I suppose?'

'You are quite mistaken. The person in question is a young and pretty girl.'

'A girl? Oho, Hugo Karlovich, and what sort of mischief have you been getting up to, I wonder?'

'Mischief?' he asked, and with a shake of his head went on 'Mischief there has not been, and mischief there could not be. This is all a very serious, clear-cut and substantial affair, which hinge upon my acquiring the sum of three thousand thalers. Then you will see me . . .'

'Upon the very peak of happiness?'

'Well, not quite . . . not on the peak, I mean, but not far off. The peak of happiness I shall attain only when I have saved ten thousand thalers.'

'Isn't what you are trying to say simply that you are planning to get married, and that in your town of Doberan or somewhere nearby there is a nice, good-looking girl, who also has some fraction of your own iron will?'

'Yes, precisely. You are quite correct.'

'And the two of you, as befits people of truly strong will, have solemnly agreed to put off the wedding until such time as you have accumulated three thousand thalers?'

'That's it exactly! How well you have guessed!'

'Well,' I said, 'there wasn't much guesswork required!'

'But listen, do you think, given your national character, that you Russians would be capable of such a thing?'

'Oh come on, let's not go on about the Russian character. How can we hope to sit and drink tea with you, when we can't even wrinkle our noses the way you do?'

'Incidentally,' he said, 'you haven't guessed quite the whole story.'

'Oh, what else then?'

'Well you see, it involves an important exercise for the will, a very, very important exercise, for which I am constantly training myself.'

'Keep at it, my lad, keep at it!', I thought, and I left him to write the letter to his distant fiancée.

An hour later he appeared, letter in hand, and asked me to send it off. He stayed for a glass of tea, and turned out to be in a very loquacious mood, expatiating on all his private dreams and fancies. He sat there building his castles in the air, and all the time smiling, as though he had actually caught sight of the crock of gold at the rainbow's end. The wretched fellow was so enraptured that I could hardly stand the sight of him, and I felt the urge to stick a little pin in him somewhere. It was a temptation I could not in the end resist; so when Hugo for no apparent reason put his arm round my shoulders and enquired whether I could imagine what the progeny would be like of a union between a highly self-controlled woman and an equally self-controlled man, I replied:

'I can.'

'Well, what do you imagine?'

'I imagine there might not be any.'

Pectoralis looked at me, pop-eyed, and asked:

'What makes you say that?'

I took pity and replied that I had simply been joking.

'I see; you were joking. But this is no joking matter. It could indeed be as you say: but it would be a very, very important matter, requiring the ultimate degree of iron will.'

'The devil take you', I thought to myself. 'I wouldn't even try to guess what wondrous notions you have in mind.' Actually, I could never have guessed, even if I *had* tried.

VI

In the meantime Pectoralis's iron will, which had brought us real benefits in those aspects of his work where persistence was at a premium, and to which he looked for such important benefits in his own life – this same iron will continued to be looked upon by us, in our simple Russian way, as something of a joke and an amusement. Frankly, no matter how surprising it may seem, we had little choice: for that was precisely the way it was turning out to be.

As a man whose obstinacy and doggedness knew no bounds, Pectoralis was obstinate in every last little thing, dogged and unyielding not just in matters of importance, but in trifles too. He exercised his will in the same way that other people do gymnastics, simply to develop strength: he exercised it systematically and unrelentingly, as though he were fulfilling some mission in life. The famous victories he won over himself rendered him dangerously smug, and from time to time led him into either highly unfortunate, or utterly hilarious, situations. Thus, for instance, by the application of his iron will, he was learning Russian with extraordinary speed and precision; but before he could master the language completely, he already began to suffer for it as a consequence of that same iron will. His sufferings, moreover, were corporeal and severe, to the extent that he did himself actual physical injury – the ultimate effects of which were fairly serious.

Pectoralis had sworn to acquire a complete, grammatically impeccable knowledge of Russian in six months, and thereupon, on a day fixed in advance, to begin speaking it. He was aware that Germans trying to speak Russian sound funny: *he* did not wish to be funny. He studied on his own, without guidance, and, what's more, in secret, so that none of us had any inkling of what he was up to. Prior to the appointed day, Pectoralis uttered not a single word of Russian. He even gave the impression of having forgotten the few words he once knew: 'possible', 'impossible', 'customs' and 'travel warrant'. Then suddenly, one fine morning, he came into my room and declared, albeit haltingly and not entirely correctly, yet in a fairly good accent:

'Well, good day! How are you?'

'Good Heavens, Hugo Karlovich!' I replied, 'You've certainly caught me bending!'

'Caught you bending?' he repeated with furrowed brow. Then the penny dropped. 'Ah yes, quite so, quite so. You were, ahem . . . surprised, I dare say?'

'Surprised is hardly the word,' I answered. 'Fancy you suddenly bursting into speech like that!'

'But it had to be like that.'

'Why "had to be"? Did the gift of tongues suddenly descend on you or something?'

Once again he paused for thought, repeating to himself: "Gift of tongs" – and sank into silent puzzlement.

'The gift of *tongues*,' I repeated.

Pectoralis immediately saw his error and answered in perfect Russian: 'Oh no, not a gift, but . . .'

'Your iron will, I suppose!'

Pectoralis levelled a dignified finger at his own chest and replied: 'Quite so, precisely.'

He thereupon informed me in the friendliest possible manner that he had always harboured the intention of mastering Russian, because, although he had remarked that certain compatriots of his managed to live in Russia without a proper knowledge of the language, he felt that that was possible only for those in government service, whereas he, as an independent professional man, was obliged to do things differently.

'It's absolutely vital,' he went on. 'You'll never get anywhere otherwise: and I don't want to let anyone get the better of me.'

I felt like saying, 'My dear fellow, when the time comes, language or no language, you'll still get plucked', but I didn't want to spoil his mood. Let the fellow enjoy himself!

From that time on Pectoralis addressed all Russians in their own tongue; and, although he made mistakes, if his mistake was such as to cause him to say something he didn't mean, then, regardless of what it might cost him, he bore the consequences with great fortitude, and by applying the full force of his iron will, stuck religiously to his word. It was now that he began to pay the penalty for this smug self-control. A man who insists upon doing everything his own way, whatever the cost, becomes willy-nilly the slave of others – and, what's more, doesn't even notice what is happening. So it was with Pectoralis. Fearing to lose face, even in the slightest degree, he ended up doing things he did not, and could not, wish to do: but nothing would induce him to admit it.

It didn't take long for people to see what was going on, and poor Pectoralis was made the victim of all manner of nasty pranks. He got into trouble with his Russian primarily when he had to make some rapid reply, and he often finished up by saying precisely the opposite of what he meant.

For instance, someone would ask: 'Hugo Karlovich, how do you want your tea, a touch weaker or a touch stronger?'

Failing to grasp immediately what was meant by 'a touch this or that', he would reply: 'A touch stronger; yes, a touch stronger.'

'More than a touch, perhaps?'

'Oh yes, please, more than a touch.'

'Maybe, a touch stronger even than that?'

'Yes, a touch stronger even.'

He would thereupon be poured a glass of tea as black as pitch, with the enquiry: 'Isn't that a bit strong for you?'

Hugo would perceive that the tea was very strong indeed, and not at all what he wanted, but his iron will would not permit him to admit as much.

'No, no, it's fine,' he would answer, swallowing the vile brew. When his companions expressed their surprise that he, a German, could stomach such strong tea, he replied brashly that he was very fond of it like that.

'You mean you really like it?' they would say.

'Oh, I'm absolutely frightfully fond of it,' he would reply.

'But it's very bad for you, you know.'

'No, no, not in the least.'

'Really you know, one might think that . . . perhaps . . .'

'Perhaps what?'

'Perhaps . . . you said something you didn't intend.'

'Whatever next!'

Despite the fact that he could not abide strong tea, he continued to assert that he liked it 'frightfully': as a result everyone around vied in filling him up with this popular Russian beverage, to the extent that it became a regular instrument of torture. Still he would not capitulate; and he continued to drink neat theine in place of tea until one fine day he suffered a nervous fit.

The wretched German lay prostrate and speechless for about a week, but when the gift of speech was restored, his first whispered utterance was on the subject of his iron will.

Emerging from his illness, he stretched out a feeble hand, grasped my own, and confessed: 'I'm well content with myself.'

'And what are you so pleased about, pray?'

'I did not let myself down,' he said; but he did not specify precisely what act of self-control afforded him such satisfaction.

That marked the end of his torture by tea. He gave up tea-drinking, since the doctors had expressly forbidden it, and the only way he could keep face was by putting on a show of missing it. However, it wasn't long before exactly the same thing happened to him again with a particular brand of French mustard. I don't recollect precisely, but probably as the result of an incident similar to the one with the tea, Hugo Karlovich acquired the reputation of a fanatical devotee of this special brand of French mustard. It was consequently served to him with every dish, and the poor fellow ate it, even spreading it on his bread like butter, all the time proclaiming that it was extraordinarily tasty and that he was 'frightfully' fond of it.

The mustard experiment produced the same results as had the tea: Pectoralis nearly died of acute stomach catarrh; and although the illness was checked, it nonetheless caused damage which affected the unfortunate stoic until the very day of his tragi-comic death.

There were plenty of other such hilarious and, at the same time, pathetic incidents involving Pectoralis: I cannot hope to remember and relate all of them. However, there do stick in my memory three occasions when Hugo, ever the victim of his own iron will, nonetheless found it impossible to assert that things were as he wanted them to be.

This was a stage in his career when he was destined first to reach an apogee, and then, after tottering a while, to plunge to disaster.

VII

It all began when, during his first summer with us, Hugo invented an unusual carriage for his private use. I should just mention that from where we lived to the town was some forty versts by road, but there was a forest track which halved the length of the journey. Mind you, this track was practically impassable; it was only the peasants who managed to negotiate it in their little two-wheel carts, and then with some difficulty. Hugo wanted to make use of this short cut, but didn't fancy rattling about in a peasant cart: so he cobbled together for his own purposes something rather like a chariot. It consisted of an ordinary armchair with a sprung base, mounted on a frame, and the whole thing bolted to the front half of an old droshky. This ingenious contraption looked so odd that the peasants, espying Pectoralis perched upon it, christened him 'God of the Mordvinians'.* As if that were not bad enough, the armchair, deprived of its customary sitting-room tranquillity, displayed no affection whatsoever for the road; it found the bumping and shaking hard to bear, and frequently leapt from its frame, as a result of which Hugo's horse not infrequently trotted home alone, to be followed an hour or two later by its wretched owner, who trudged in humping his armchair upon his back. He did not always escape so lightly: on one occasion he together with his armchair toppled into a bog, where he duly sat until he was hauled out and carried home in a thoroughly pitiful condition.

Even Hugo found it impossible to assert that this was something he had wanted to happen: what *was* possible was to insist on doing everything his own way, to refuse ever to abandon his own mulishness – and these things he did with astonishing persistence.

This is what happened on another occasion. One day Hugo, who had just been out hunting and was soaked to the skin, was dragged by one of our principals to the tea table, at which our entire colony had gathered to while away the evening in friendly conversation. He was poured a glass of hot water and red wine, and asked what success he had had in the field. Now he was a good hunter and didn't tell many fisherman's tales; but since in this as in all things his iron will had its part to play, the tale he told, though entirely guileless, interested and amused us. We were all listening and enjoying the fun, when suddenly, to our considerable annoyance, wasps began appearing and buzzing around the room, thus disrupting our comfortable colloquy. It was all very odd – indeed, quite incomprehensible: where on earth were they coming from? The windows were open, it was true; but a fine summer drizzle was falling, making it impossible for these vicious little bugs to fly. So where *could* they be coming from? Yet they kept buzzing round, popping up like flowers from a conjuror's hat: they crawled up the table legs, across the tablecloth and the plates, then on to Hugo's back – until finally one of them stung the young lady of the house most painfully on the hand.

It was quite impossible to continue our conversation: a hubbub ensued, in which the apprehensiveness of the ladies and the solicitude of the men combined to create a regular shambles. The situation required counter-measures of the most energetic kind: everyone began to rush about, some waving handkerchiefs, others chasing the wasps with napkins, while yet others dived for cover. The only person to remain aloof from all this frenetic activity was Hugo, and he had his reasons . . . He stood alone, motionless, next to the chair upon which he had hitherto been seated, and presenting a hideous and pitiful figure: his face was dreadfully pale, his lips were quivering, and his hands were twitching convulsively: meanwhile, the whole of his frock-coat, which was still quite damp, and particularly the back of it, was alive with wasps.

'Great heavens!' we exclaimed, examining him from all sides, 'you're a real wasp's nest and no mistake, Hugo Karlovich.'

'Oh no,' he replied, articulating each word with some difficulty, 'I am not a nest, but I have a nest.'

'A wasp's nest?'

'Yes. I found it, but it was wet – and I wanted to examine it, so I brought it home with me.'

'And where is it now?'

'In my back pocket.'

'So that's it!'

We ripped off his coat (the ladies having long since fled this dangerous spot) and found that the back of Hugo's waistcoat was swarming with wasps, which were crawling upwards and, as they got warmer, spreading their wings and taking to the air. Meanwhile, from his pockets more were emerging in an unbroken chain.

The first thing we did, of course, was to throw Hugo's ill-fated coat on the floor and trample to pulp the wasps' nest that had caused all the fuss: then we turned our attention to Hugo himself. He had been stung to bits, but had uttered not a single complaint, not a single sound. We brushed off all the wasps crawling inside his shirt, smeared him from head to toe with oil, like a sausage, put him on a sofa and pulled a sheet over him. He rapidly turned puffy all over and was obviously suffering agonies: but when one of the Englishmen, feeling sorry for him, remarked that this man was indeed endowed with an iron will, Hugo smiled and, turning towards us, uttered reproachfully: 'How glad I am that you no longer doubt it.'

We left him to enjoy his iron will and said no more to him – while he, poor fellow, had no idea what an object of general derision he had become. Meanwhile, another adventure was awaiting him.

VIII

I should mention at this point that Hugo, though not actually mean, was, to say the least, extremely money-wise and thrifty: and since his thriftiness was aimed at the quickest possible accumulation of the required three thousand thalers, and, in the pursuit of this aim, was fortified by a will of iron, then it could hardly be distinguished from the most outrageous miserliness. He denied himself absolutely everything which he could conceivably do without. He did not have his clothes cleaned and mended; and, since he kept no servants, he polished his own boots. There was, however, one item on which he was obliged to loosen his purse strings, if only because rational economic principles demanded it. Considering hired horses an extravagance, Hugo decided to get a horse of his own; but he set about it in a curious way. There were any number of stud-farms in our neighbourhood, both large and small: but among the local horse-breeders one stood out – a certain Dmitry Yerofeich, the owner of a medium-sized estate and a bit of a character. No one could match this Dmitry Yerofeich when it came to fobbing off a dud horse on someone: moreover, when he swindled you, he did it not like some common-or-garden horse trader, but like an artist – more for swank, for the sheer fun of it and to maintain his reputation. The more the buyer was known as, or pretended to be, an expert on horses, the more boldly and impudently Dmitry Yerofeich cheated him. The joy which an encounter with such an 'expert' afforded him defies description: he would begin with compliments – for instance, that it was a great pleasure to do business with a man who knew what he was talking about. Then he'd put on a show of complete guilelessness: he wouldn't praise the horse; instead, he'd say in a half-contemptuous tone:

'A decent sort of nag, but nothing very special, not the sort you'd send to a show; but then, there it is, you can see for yourself.'

The expert would then look at the horse; meanwhile, Dmitry Yerofeich would shout at the groom:

'Don't keep pulling her round like that! What do you think you're doing, twisting about like a devil before matins? We're not gypsies, for God's sake let the gentleman look her over, stand her quietly. By the way, that lameness in her leg – she's sound again now, is she?'

'What lameness was that?' the purchaser would enquire.

'Oh, she had some problem with a pastern.'

'That wasn't this horse, Dmitry Yerofeich,' the groom would say.

'Not this one? Oh well, damn it, I can't remember all of them. Now, sir, you take a good hard look, so you don't make any mistakes. She's going cheap, to be sure, but still, you don't want to waste your money, do you? – money's never cheap, when all's said and done. Now if you'll forgive me, I'm feeling a little tired and I think I'll go home.'

He would thereupon depart, leaving the buyer in his absence to examine all the more attentively the horse's pastern – which had indeed suffered no injury whatsoever – and in doing so, overlook all the horse's real defects.

Having completed the crooked deal, Dmitry Yerofeich would say, cool as a cucumber:

'Business is business – and you should know better than to show off how clever you are. Let this be a lesson to you for your boasting.'

Even so, Dmitry Yerofeich had his Achilles heel, a chink in his armour. Just as every man aspires to that which he does not deserve, so Dmitry Yerofeich yearned for people to take him at his word. It was a long-standing weakness, which he had framed in the solemn formula: 'Ask me no questions, and I'll tell you no lies. Trust in me, not in what you see. Then I'll give you an honest deal: for a hundred I'll let you have a horse worth five times the price.'

And he would indeed be as good as his word: for Dmitry Yerofeich it was a point of honour, a test of his own brand of iron will. However, since a good proportion of his customers took advantage of it, it cost Dmitry Yerofeich a fair amount of money – and for some time he had wanted to get out of this tiresome business of doing deals on trust. For a long time he couldn't bring himself to do it, but when the gods sent Pectoralis his way, Dmitry Yerofeich finally took the plunge. Barely had Hugo opened his mouth to say he needed a horse and to ask Dmitry Yerofeich to do the deal on trust, than the latter replied:

'My dear chap, what sort of trust is there nowadays! I've got plenty of horses; take a look, choose one for yourself as you know best, and never mind about trust!'

'Oh come, Dmitry Yerofeich, I trust you completely, I know I can rely on you.'

'Well, you take my tip, my lad: don't trust anyone and don't rely on anyone. What's the point of relying on others, eh? Are you such a fool that you can't trust yourself?'

'Look, say what you will, but my mind's made up. Here's a hundred roubles, take it and give me a horse. Surely you can't refuse me that?'

'Refuse? Why should I refuse? A hundred roubles is a hundred roubles, when all's said and done, and why should I turn it down? It's just that I don't like the idea that you might regret the deal.'

'I shall not regret it.'

'How can you be so sure? After all, it isn't money you've come by easily – you've earned every penny by the sweat of your brow. If I give you a dud horse, you'll regret it all right, and you'll start complaining.'

'I shall not complain.'

'You're just saying that; how could you not complain? If you think you've had a bad deal, you'll not keep silent.'

'I give you my word that I shall never complain, not to anyone.'

'You'll swear to that?'

'Dmitry Yerofeich, where I come from, people don't swear oaths.'

'Oh, I see, so you don't swear oaths, don't you? Well then, how am I supposed to believe you?'

'You can believe my iron will.'

'Have it your own way then,' decided Dmitry Yerofeich, and, having entertained Pectoralis to supper, called his groom and said: 'Harness up Okrysa to Hugo Karlovich's sledge.'

'Okrysa, Dmitry Yerofeich?' replied the astonished groom.

'Yes, Okrysa.'

'You mean, harness up . . . Okrysa?'

'For God's sake, what do you keep asking the same question for, you fool? I said: harness her up, and that's what I mean.' And turning with a smile to Pectoralis, he said: 'Brother, it's a magnificent beast I'm letting you have, a young mare, a palomino, of superb conformation. Her coat is a wonder to behold. I guarantee she'll be a horse you'll never forget.'

'I'm obliged to you,' said Pectoralis, 'very much obliged.'

'When you've driven her a bit, then you'll thank me; mind you, if there turns out to be anything about her which doesn't suit you, just you remember your promise: no cursing, no complaining – after all, I have no way of knowing exactly what sort of horse you were looking for.'

'I shall never complain to anyone. I have already said as much, and you may rely on my iron will.'

'Well, if that's the case, you're a splendid fellow and no mistake. For my part, brother, I've no will-power at all. How many times have I tried to make up my mind to give everyone a fair deal, but I still can't seem to stick to it. And once a man does something, well, even if he goes and confesses it to the priest, that won't put the matter right. But I suppose you Lutherans don't go in for confessions, come to that?'

'We confess only to God.'

'Now that's will-power for you: no swearing oaths and no confessions! But then of course you don't have priests, or saints either, for that matter. Come to think of it, how could you have saints, when they're all Russian anyway. Cheerio, my good fellow; you jump in and take a drive. I'm off to say my prayers and go to bed.'

Whereupon they parted.

Pectoralis knew Dmitry Yerofeich to be a bit of a wag, and was convinced that this talk was all in jest. He put on his coat, went out on to the porch, got into his sledge, but had scarcely touched the reins when the horse shot forward and charged head-first into a wall. He pulled her round: whereupon she again leapt away and ran headlong into a barn door, hitting herself so hard that she stood there tossing her head in pain.

Our German friend was bewildered, but could find no one from whom he might seek an explanation, because while this had been going on, all traces of life in Dmitry Yerofeich's house had suddenly vanished; the lights had all gone out and the servants had disappeared somewhere. It was like an enchanted castle: no sign of life, only the moonlight shining on the fields beyond the gates, and a crisp, crackling frost.

Hugo, looking around, saw that he was in a pretty pickle. He turned the horse to face the moon, and recoiled in fright: the distended, clouded eyeballs of the hapless Okrysa gazed unblinking at the moon, glassy and lifeless as two small foggy mirrors. The moonlight gave them a metallic sheen.

'She's blind.' As the fact dawned upon him, Hugo once more cast a glance around the yard.

In the moonlight he thought he glimpsed at one of the windows the tall figure of Dmitry Yerofeich, who had presumably not yet gone to bed, but was admiring the moon and perhaps preparing to say his prayers. Hugo fetched a sigh, took the horse by the bridle and led her from the yard: no sooner had the gates been closed behind him than a small light appeared in Dmitry

Yerofeich's window: no doubt the old man had lit his icon-lamp and begun his prayers.

IX

Poor Hugo, cruelly, pitilessly deceived, suffering agonies of resentment, intolerable frustration and loss, hopelessly stranded amidst the empty fields, bore it all and bore it bravely. For forty versts he plodded alongside the blind horse, behind which trailed his empty sledge. What, you might ask, did he do with all these accumulated emotions, and with the horse? No one ever saw the horse again, nor did he ever tell what became of it (he probably sold it to the Tatars in Ishim). As for Dmitry Yerofeich, whose house was a regular stopping-off place for all our company – Pectoralis went on visiting him as before, and in his relations with him betrayed not the slightest sign of discontent. True, Dmitry Yerofeich did his best for a long time to avoid him, but when they finally came face to face, Pectoralis did not even mention the horse.

In the end Dmitry Yerofeich could bear it no longer and broached the topic himself.

'By the way,' he said, 'I've been meaning to ask, how do you like the horse?'

'Oh, she's fine, just fine,' answered Pectoralis.

'Well, naturally, that goes without saying, she's a fine animal; but how do you find her to drive?'

'She's fine to drive.'

'That *is* splendid news. I never doubted she'd be good in harness. But tell me, why aren't you using her today?'

'Oh, I like to use her sparingly.'

'Absolutely right. Very wise of you. You take good care of her, my friend; a marvellous mare like that, she deserves to be taken care of.'

And while he went around telling his staff in an eminently good-natured tone that Hugo Karlovich had found their dear old

Okrysa very much to his liking, he thought to himself: 'By God, he's a weird devil, that German. It's the first time in my life I can remember swindling a man till his eyes popped, and him not cursing nor even complaining.'

Dmitry Yerofeich ended up getting quite worried about the whole affair. He couldn't fathom what was going on, and eventually began telling everyone how he had cheated Pectoralis, and desperately seeking to discover why Pectoralis would not complain. But Pectoralis stuck to his guns, and when he found out what Dmitry Yerofeich was saying, merely shrugged his shoulders and commented:

'No self-control, that's his trouble.'

Rascal though Dmitry Yerofeich was, he lacked nerve, and was a devout and superstitious man. He imagined that Pectoralis was planning some frightfully devious, calculated revenge, and, to quell his own anxiety, sent him a marvellous horse worth about three hundred roubles, together with his respects and a plea for forgiveness.

Pectoralis blushed, but without hesitation ordered the horse to be sent back with no reply, and then wrote to Dmitry Yerofeich: 'I'm ashamed for you: you've got no will-power.'

Then suddenly this extraordinary fellow who before our eyes had subjected his will to so many trials, found himself on the verge of realizing his ambition. The New Year brought him a further increase in salary, which, when added to his savings, swept him past his target of three thousand thalers.

Thanking his masters, he immediately packed his bags for Germany, and promised to return with his wife in a month's time.

His preparations for the trip did not take long. He departed, and we began to look forward to his return with his new wife, who, we all imagined, was bound to turn out to be something very special.

But special in what way?

'A special swindle, my lads, that's what she'll be,' Dmitry Yerofeich did his best to persuade us.

X

It wasn't long before we had news from Pectoralis. A month after his departure he wrote to tell me that he had married. He referred to his wife by her 'Russian' name, Klara Pavlovna. After another month he graced us once more with his company, this time together with his spouse, whom, I confess, we had all been dying to see and eyed, therefore, with undisguised curiosity.

Knowing as we did in our little colony all Pectoralis's quirks, both large and small, we were convinced to the last man that his marriage too would turn out to be freakish in some way or other.

And so, as we shall see, it turned out to be: it was, however, some time before we grasped what was going on.

Klara Pavlovna was a fairly typical German woman – big and, by all accounts, healthy, though with a rather haemorrhoidal flush to her face, and one real curiosity of physique – the whole left side of her body was considerably more bulky than the right. This was particularly noticeable in her rather swollen left cheek, which looked permanently abscessed, and in her extremities. Both her left hand and left foot were distinctly larger than her right ones.

It was Hugo himself who drew our attention to this: indeed he seemed to take pride in it.

'Look,' he would say, 'this hand is larger, this one smaller. You don't come across that very often.'

It was the first time I had ever encountered this strange trick of nature, and I felt sorry for poor Hugo in that he would always have to buy two pairs of shoes or gloves for his wife instead of one. My sympathy, however, was wasted, since Madame Pectoralis had her own way of dealing with the problem: she chose shoes and gloves of the larger size, as a result of which one shoe always fitted, while the other kept falling off. The same thing happened with her gloves.

None of us much cared for this lady, who, to be honest, was so coarse and common that she scarcely merited the title 'lady' at all. Many of us couldn't help wondering what it was that Pectoralis found in this strapping, vulgar *Frau* in the first place; was she really worth all the vows he had taken in order to marry her? And then he had gone so far to fetch her, all the way to Germany . . . We sometimes felt like singing to him:

> What the devil made you roam?
> We'd soon have married you at home.*

Obviously he must have chosen her for some moral or spiritual virtues – strength of will, for instance. We enquired about that too: 'Does Klara Pavlovna have a strong will?'

Pectoralis pulled a wry face and replied: 'Devilishly strong!'

Klara Pavlovna was entirely unsuited to the society of our English ladies, many of whom were very intelligent and refined; both she and Pectoralis sensed the fact. Hugo, mind you, didn't care a jot: indeed, it was of no concern to him what anyone thought of his wife. Like a true German, he kept her, not to suit his masters, but to satisfy his own needs, and he felt no embarrassment at her being so out of place in the society in which she found herself. She did have what he needed, and what he valued above all else – an iron will, which in conjunction with his own was guaranteed to produce wondrous offspring – and that was enough for him!

It came as something of a surprise, therefore, that no one seemed to see any signs of this will-power of hers. Klara Pectoralis lived the life of any ordinary *Hausfrau*: she cooked her husband soup, fried him meatballs and knitted him socks and stockings; and when her husband was working away from home – which at that time was quite often – she would sit with the mechanic Offenberg, an extraordinarily stupid, wooden German from Sarepta,* who worked as Pectoralis's assistant.

A dozen words will suffice to describe Offenberg. He was a young fellow, who would have served as an admirable model for any actor playing the part of the workman seduced by his mistress in that well-known trifle *The Miller's Wife from Marly*.* We all thought him a simpleton, though there was, mind you, something calculating, an element of honeyed cunning about him, characteristic of those simple folk whom one encounters in Jesuit houses in the Rue de Sèvres and other places.

Offenberg had been hired to help Pectoralis, not so much as a mechanic as in the role of an interpreter, to give instructions to the workforce; however, he had turned out to be not much good in this capacity either, and often got things in a muddle. Still, Pectoralis put up with him, and found some use for him even after he had learned to speak Russian for himself. Not only that: for some reason Pectoralis had taken a liking to the idiotic Offenberg and used to spend his leisure hours with him: he shared rooms with him, slept – until his marriage, that is – in the same bedroom, played chess and went hunting with him, and kept a close watch on his moral behaviour, as though he had been particularly entrusted with that task by Offenberg's parents or the elders of the Sarepta branch of the Moravian Brethren. Offenberg and Pectoralis, then, had lived as good friends and had very rarely been seen apart. Now all that had changed, because Pectoralis's work frequently took him away from home. Not that this new situation offered any threat at all to Offenberg's moral character, which Frau Klara, in her husband's absence, now kept under unremitting scrutiny. This was a mutually advantageous situation. Offenberg kept Frau Klara from getting bored, while she protected him from all the enticements and temptations to which the young are susceptible. This too was a sensible, carefully considered arrangement; but it caught the Devil's eye, and he made a proper monkey of it: all of which – thanks to the upright and eccentric character of our fine friend Hugo – precipitated a notorious scandal and turned the whole household on its head.

According to the womenfolk, the whole episode which I will now relate was the unforgivable fault of Hugo himself: but then, do the ladies ever lay the blame other than at the husband's door? Listen with an impartial ear, I beg you, to what I have to tell, and form your own opinion, without any prompting from the ladies.

XI

A year had passed since Pectoralis's marriage, then a second, and finally a third. Indeed, so might also have passed a sixth, an eighth and a tenth, had not the third year turned out for Pectoralis particularly fortunate from the financial point of view. This good fortune brought about a major misfortune, of which you will hear forthwith.

I have, I think, already stated that Pectoralis had a thoroughly sound mastery of his trade; this, together with that meticulousness which was his hallmark and that dogged persistence which stemmed from his iron will, combined to ensure that every single thing he undertook to do, he did conscientiously and well. He was soon widely known throughout the district, and he was constantly being invited to one place or another to set up, repair or adjust various bits of machinery. Our principals imposed no restraints upon this activity; Hugo managed to fit in all these odd jobs and earned a good deal of money in the process. His resources were growing at such a rate that he began to consider whether he should not resign his position with the firm in Doberan and set up his own engineering works in the heart of our industrial region, in the town of R.

This was a perfectly simple and understandable ambition; after all, who would not find it desirable to give up being paid by the hour and become his own boss? However, Hugo Karlovich had other strong motives for making this change: the acquisition of his own business he saw as a logical extension of his rules of life. Now I dare say you don't quite see what I mean by that, but I am obliged for the moment to keep the explanation under my hat.

I don't honestly recall exactly how much money Pectoralis reckoned he needed to set up his own factory, but it was about twelve or fifteen thousand roubles, I think. Anyway, no sooner had he put the last kopeck of the required sum into his account than he drew a line under one period of his life and announced the beginning of a fresh one.

This fresh start was accomplished in three stages, the first of which consisted in Pectoralis's announcing that he was giving up his job and opening a works in the town. The second stage was the setting up of the factory, which meant first of all acquiring a site, preferably one that was cheap and conveniently located. In a small town there weren't many sites like that, and of those that existed only one answered all Pectoralis's requirements: that was the one he went for. It was a large patch of low-lying ground between the market square and the river; upon it there already stood some big old stone buildings, which could be adapted to his purpose at minimal cost. Unfortunately, half of this site which had caught Pectoralis's fancy had been for some years rented on a long-term lease to Safronych, the proprietor of the small iron-foundry. Pectoralis knew the foundry and its proprietor, and he hoped he could shift them. True, Safronych did not encourage him in this hope, and even stated quite openly that he wouldn't leave the place. Pectoralis thereupon devised a plan which he reckoned Safronych would have no answer to. Placing his trust in this plan, Pectoralis duly bought the site and one fine day came back to his old haunts to see us, bearing the deeds of purchase and in a distinctly euphoric mood. He was in such high spirits that he allowed himself some considerable and thoroughly uncharacteristic extravagances, openly embracing his wife, kissing both his principals, tweaking Offenberg's ears, and finally announcing that he had set himself up in business, that he thanked us for our hospitality and that he would be departing promptly to take up his affairs in the town of R.

I got the impression that Klara Pavlovna paled at this news, and Offenberg became so flustered that even Hugo couldn't help noticing it and remarked, roaring with laughter: 'O–ho, you weren't expecting that, were you, you dummy?'

And so saying, he turned the wooden *Herrnhuter** towards him, slapped him on the shoulder and added: 'Never mind, don't you fret, Offenberg. I haven't forgotten you: I shan't leave you behind, you'll stay with me; but now off with you to the town, and bring back plenty of champagne and the rest of the stuff I've bought: it's all on this bit of paper.'

The note in question listed a whole range of things which Pectoralis had purchased and left in town for collection – wine, *zakuski** and so on.

Pectoralis obviously planned to treat us to a real feast, and, sure enough, the very next day, when all the provisions had arrived, he went round inviting all of us that evening to a celebration to mark his marriage.

I thought perhaps I had misheard him and asked:

'You mean you're giving a farewell dinner to mark your departure and your new business venture?'

'No, no; we'll celebrate that on the spot, when the business really gets going; but I'm having a party now to mark the fact that today I shall be married.'

'What? Married, today?'

'Yes, yes, indeed: today Klara Pavlovna will . . . I shall be marrying her today.'

'What nonsense is this?'

'There's no nonsense; I'm definitely getting married.'

'How can you get married? For goodness sake, you've been married for three years already.'

'Hm, yes, three years, three years. There, you see! You think things are bound to go on in the same way as they have for the last three years! Well, of course, things could have gone on like that for *thirty*–three years, if I hadn't got the money together and started my own business: but now, my dear chap, that's not the case. Yes, Klara Pavlovna, have no fear, my love, this very day I shall make you my bride. You still don't take my meaning?'

'I'm completely foxed.'

'Why, it's perfectly simple. Klarinka and I agreed to wed only when I had saved three thousand thalers. Only the ceremony, you understand, nothing more . . . but when I became my own boss, then we would be properly married. Now do you see?'

'Good grief,' I said, 'I'm sorry to say, for your sake, that I am beginning to see – that the two of you . . . for fully three years . . . have refrained from . . . being married!'

'Yes, quite so, I've still not . . . married her! Well, I did tell you, didn't I, that if I hadn't managed to set myself up in business, I would have gone on that way for thirty-three years.'

'You're an astounding fellow!'

'Yes, yes, yes, I'm well aware that I'm an astounding fellow – I have a will of iron! Did you really not grasp what I told you long ago, that when I had saved three thousand thalers, I should still not reach the actual peak of happiness, but only come close to it?'

'No,' I replied, 'at that time I did not grasp your meaning.'

'And now you do?'

'Now I do.'

'You're a wise fellow, to be sure. And what do you think about me now? I'm my own master now and I can have my own family. I shall have everything I want.'

'Well done,' I said, 'well done! . . . By the devil, you have done well!'

For the rest of that day, right until the evening, I was genuinely disturbed by this extraordinary turn of events.

'The Teutonic fiend!' I thought. 'He could beat our Chichikov at his own game.'

And just as Heine suffered the recurrent nightmare of a black Prussian eagle carrying off Germany in its talons, so in my mind's eye I kept seeing this German who was preparing that day, after three years of marriage, at last to be a husband to his wife.

Well, I ask you, after that, what might not such a man endure or achieve?

I was plagued by this question during the whole course of the celebratory dinner, which turned out to be a lengthy and bounteous affair, at which Russians, Englishmen and Germans all alike got drunk, exchanged kisses and dropped unsubtle hints to Pectoralis about how this merrymaking might rob him of those long-awaited moments of bliss. Pectoralis, however, was not to be moved. He too was tipsy, but kept saying:

'I'm in no hurry. I never hurry, but I get everything done in the end, and everything comes my way in its own good time. Please, sit and drink. Don't forget, I have an iron will.'

At that moment the wretched fellow was still blissfully unaware of how much he would need that iron will of his, and what trials awaited it.

XII

Thanks to this splendid dinner I overslept on the following morning by a good half hour, and even then I didn't feel much like getting up, despite the most persistent efforts of the servant who came in to wake me. What finally compelled me to make the effort was the news that he brought with him – news which it took me some little time to comprehend.

It concerned Hugo Karlovich – which led me to wonder whether the drunken orgy he had thrown on the previous night was still going on.

'What's it all about?' I said, sitting on the edge of my bed and peering somnolently at my servant.

What it was about was this: an hour after his last guest had departed, in the grey of the dawn, Hugo had emerged on to the porch of the wing in which he lived, given a piercing whistle and shouted: 'Well!'

A few moments later he shouted the same thing again in a louder voice, then began yelling it over and over again, louder and louder: 'Well! Well!'

A nightwatchman went up to him and enquired: 'Is there anything I can do, sir?'

'Yes, go this minute and fetch me Mr "Well!"'

The nightwatchman observed the German for a moment, then replied: 'Look, old fellow, go and get some sleep; you don't know what you're saying.'

'Be quiet, you fool, and send me Mr "Well!". Go on, be off with you, to the mechanics' quarters, find his room, wake him up and tell him to get over here straightaway.'

'Ugh, they're sozzled, the heathens!' thought the watchman to himself, and decided to go and rouse Offenberg: after all, he was a German, so he might have some chance of sorting out what this other German fellow was on about.

Offenberg was also a bit under the weather and had a job forcing his eyes open: still, he got up, dressed and set off to find Pectoralis, who, while all this was going on, remained standing on the porch in his slippers. When Offenberg hove into sight, Pectoralis shuddered and yelled once more: 'Well!'

'What do you want?' asked Offenberg.

'Well . . . what I want . . . Well . . . that doesn't exist any more,' replied Pectoralis. And in an altogether more threatening tone, he ordered: 'You just follow me!'

Offenberg followed him to his house, where Pectoralis led him into the office and locked the door behind them. Since that moment, the servant said, they had been fighting.

I couldn't believe my ears. My servant, however, assured me that it was true and added that the fight was no joking matter: the door was locked, so no one could see what was going on, neither combatant was uttering a sound, and all you could hear was the terrible thudding of fists and the wailing of the lady of the house.

'You really should get over there,' he said. 'The other gentlemen are there already; they're afraid there may be bloodshed, but they can't get in.'

I rushed over to Pectoralis's house and there indeed found the whole of our colony assembled, in a highly agitated state, and crowding round Pectoralis's door. The door was, as I had been told, firmly locked, while behind it something quite extraordinary was going on. One could clearly detect the sound of hectic activity: somebody was dragging somebody else around the room, all the while thrashing him with some instrument or other. He would hit him, hit him again, drag him around a bit, knock him off his feet, hurl him to the floor, then thrash him some more: then there would be a sudden pause, followed by a resumption of battle to the accompaniment of quiet feminine sobbing.

'Eh, gentlemen!' people were shouting. 'Listen, that's enough. Open up!'

'Don't answer!' we heard Pectoralis say, followed immediately by the sound of further fisticuffs.

'Come on, Hugo Karlovich, call it a day!' we shouted. 'Put a stop to it, or we'll break the door down!'

Our threat seemed to work: the racket went on for a minute more, then abruptly ceased. At that very instant the catch on the door was thrown back and Offenberg came flying out, obviously not entirely unassisted.

'What's going on, Offenberg?' we all yelled in chorus, but he fled without a word.

'Hugo Karlovich, dear fellow, what on earth did you have to give him a battering like that for?'

'He knows,' replied Pectoralis, who had in fact received no less a battering than Offenberg.

'Whatever he did to offend you, it doesn't alter the fact . . . that is to say, how *could* you?'

'And why shouldn't I?'

'What, thrash a man half to death like that?'

'Oh, and why not? He was thrashing me too: we were fighting on even terms, but the Russian way.'

'You call that the Russian way?'

'Yes. I laid that down as a firm condition – that we should fight the Russian way – and no shouting either.'

'Just a minute,' we protested, 'first of all, what's all this about fighting the Russian way, and without shouting? That's just something you've dreamed up, it's got nothing to do with us Russians.'

'I mean bashing each other in the face.'

'Oh, "bashing in the face", is it? Well, it isn't only us Russians who fight like that; and in any case, what was the reason for your . . . let us say, little tiff?'

'The reason? He knows well enough,' Pectoralis replied. This ambiguous response was as close as Pectoralis came to explaining the whole tragedy of his situation, which was, no doubt, the more unpleasant for him in that it had come upon him so unexpectedly.

Not long after the 'Russian' fight between our two Germans, Pectoralis moved to the town. As he bade me farewell, he said:

'You know, I've been, well, cruelly deceived.'

Guessing what he might be hinting at, I said nothing, but Pectoralis leaned over and whispered in my ear:

'Well, my little Klara doesn't have quite the iron will I credited her with, and she made a very poor job of looking after Offenberg.'

He took his wife with him, of course, when he went; but Offenberg he left behind. The wretched fellow stayed with us until he had recovered from his 'Russian' fight: he uttered not a word of complaint about Pectoralis: all he said was that he couldn't imagine what he had done to offend.

'He called me to him, shouted: "Well!", and then "Stand up like a man and let's have a Russian fight; and if you won't thrash me, I'm going to give you a thrashing anyway." I stood there and took it for a time, then finally I started fighting back.'

'And all just because of "Well!"?'

'He didn't give me any other reason and I don't know of any.'

'Still, well . . . it's all very strange!'

'And, well . . . it's all very painful, sir,' replied Offenberg.

'And there wasn't any hanky-panky between you and Klara Pavlovna, Offenberg?'

'No sir, I swear, I didn't do any hanking or panking.'

'And you've done nothing to be ashamed of?'

'No, sir, nothing, I swear.'

Thus the whole question of whether this latterday Joseph was guilty of the crime for which he suffered remained unresolved: however, there was no question but that Pectoralis's iron will had, on this occasion, received a severe jolt, and although it is wicked to rejoice in another man's misfortune, still, I must confess, I felt a slight glow of satisfaction when I considered the shock caused to our smug and conceited German by his discovery that Klara's powers of will were not all that they might have been.

Naturally, this shock was bound to take its effect: but it was not responsible for the breaking of his iron will. That was destined to happen in a sublimely tragi-comic fashion, but under quite different, fateful circumstances – when Pectoralis engaged in a real Russian fight . . . with a real Russian.

XIII

Pectoralis's will was sufficiently strong to withstand the strain of discovering that his wife's was not. Of course, what he found particularly hard to bear was the loss of that comforting dream –

that he might see the fruit of a union between two people of equally iron will; still, with true grit, he suppressed his anguish and set about his business with redoubled zeal.

In organizing the factory, he was careful in everything he did not to betray his reputation as a man who, regardless of circumstances and in all situations, liked everything to be done his own way.

I have already mentioned that Pectoralis had acquired a site fronting on to the road, the rear half of which had been let on a long lease to the iron-founder Safronych, and that this little man stoutly resisted all efforts to squeeze him out.

The feckless, idle, happy-go-lucky Safronych continued to stand his ground, blankly refusing to budge until his lease ran out – and the courts, judging his inflexibility to be quite within the law, could not touch him.

Meanwhile he and his scruffy workforce, to say nothing of his even scruffier premises, hampered, willy-nilly, Pectoralis's well-managed business. That was not all. In another respect the situation was even more intolerable: Safronych, revelling in his rights, began swaggering about, boasting to everyone he met:

'I want nothing to do with that so-and-so German, I can tell you. I'm a patriot to my fatherland, I am, and I'm not going to budge. And if he fancies taking me to court, well, I've got a friend who used to be a clerk at the law-courts, a chap called Zhiga, who'll soon bring him to heel.'

This was more than the pompous Pectoralis could bear: in retaliation he decided to rid himself of Safronych once and for all by a plan of his own devising – to which end he had already laid a trap for the unwary muzhik.

Pectoralis appeared to have used such prudence and guile in establishing his relations with Safronych that the latter, for all his legal rights, ended up in the palm of Pectoralis's hand, and woke up to the fact only when the noose was being tightened round his neck – or at least that was the way it seemed.

This is how it all came about.

Pectoralis laboured and grew rich, while Safronych lazed, drank, and sank slowly into ruin. Having to compete with someone like Pectoralis, Safronych was going rapidly downhill and heading for certain bankruptcy, but still sat tight on his rear lot and steadfastly refused to budge.

I well recall this poor, weak-willed fellow with his typically Russian nature – inoffensive, independent and carefree.

'What's going to become of you, Vasily Safronych?' folks would say to him, pointing to the decline in his business, which was rapidly succumbing to the onslaught of Pectoralis's aggressive methods. 'Just look where your fecklessness has got you, look what a monster has sprung up right in front of your nose.'

'What on earth is all the fuss about, gentlemen?' answered Safronych jauntily. 'Why do you keep trying to frighten me with this German bogeyman? It's all a lot of nonsense: a German's not a dog, when all's said and done; even he has got to eat. I'll get by, don't you worry.'

'But he's robbing you of all your trade.'

'And what if he is? Maybe that's the way it should be, for him to do my work for me. I'm still not going to leave the old place.'

'Oh, come on, your best plan is to get out. He'll pay you compensation.'

'No, sir, with respect, I'll not go: for tell me, pray, where could I go to? Everything I possess is here; and look what the wife has got – her pots and pans, her bits and bobs – where am I going to move all that to?'

'You're talking nonsense, Safronych. What's so difficult about moving all your stuff?'

'Well, it may look easy to you, but those things of ours, they're all battered and frail. They're all right while they're standing still, but touch them and they'll fall to bits.'

'You can buy new stuff.'

'Now why should we go buying new things, wasting our money? Old things should be looked after. What you look after, God will care for too. In any case, my pal Zhiga, the clerk, he says: "My best advice to you is, don't you budge. We'll squash this German," he says, "by sitting still."'

'You just watch Zhiga doesn't lead you up the garden path.'

'Why should he do that? If he'd said it when he was sober, then of course you might have expected him, in a moment of weakness, to stretch the truth a bit: but he swears it by God even when he's drunk: "Rejoice, Safronych," he says, "for these great deeds are done not for thy ruination, but for thy glory and prosperity."'

These offensive pronouncements, like all the previous ones, reached the ears of Pectoralis, infuriated him beyond words, and finally caused him to lose his temper and play a really dirty trick.

'If he wants to test his will against mine,' Pectoralis decided, 'then I'll show whether he can squash me by sitting still! . . . Enough is enough!' exclaimed Hugo Karlovich. 'Now just watch me settle his hash.'

'He's going to settle your hash,' Safronych was informed. At which news he merely crossed himself and replied: 'Don't you worry. What God doesn't abandon, the pig can't eat. As Zhiga says: "Just wait, and he'll choke himself on us".'

'Oh, so he'll choke to death, will he?'

'Yes, he'll choke all right. Zhiga has summed it up well: "We Russians," he says, "have got meaty bodies but bony heads. We're not your German sausage, which can be chewed down to the last scrap: there's always a bit of us left over."'

This view met with general approval.

However, the very next day after this conversation took place, Safronych's wife woke him up with the words: 'Get up quickly, you lazy lump, and come and see what that German has done to you.'

'Fiddle-faddle,' replied Safronych. 'I've already told you there's bones in me as well as meat, and no pig is going to gobble me up.'

'Well, you come and look. He's nailed up the wicket, and the main gate. I got up to go down to the river to fetch water for the samovar, and what do I find? The gates are locked, there's no way to get out, and when I shout to open them, they say Hugo Karlovich has forbidden it and had them nailed up tight.'

'That's a nice trick, that is!' said Safronych, and he went out of the house, over to the fence, and tried the wicket and the main gate: just as his wife had said, they wouldn't open.

He knocked on the gate, and knocked again, but there was no response. Our bony Russian found himself trapped in his own back yard, as in a box. Vasily Safronych scrambled up on to the roof of a shed and peered over the fence: he could see the wicket and the main gate boarded up on Hugo Karlovich's side, as solid as a brick wall.

Safronych began yelling, calling in turn everyone whose name he knew in Pectoralis's house, but without response. No one offered him any help, but Hugo himself eventually emerged, smoking one of his stinking German cigars, and said:

'Well, well! And what do you propose to do now?'

Safronych took fright.

'My dear good sir,' he said to Pectoralis from his perch up on the roof, 'what's this you're doing? I mean, you're not allowed: I'm protected by my lease.'

'Well,' said Pectoralis, 'I thought I'd give you a fence for a bit of extra protection.'

There they stood, arguing the toss, one on his porch, the other on his roof.

'How do you expect me to live like this?' enquired Safronych. 'I can't get out of my yard, for goodness' sake.'

'I know. That's why I did it, so that you couldn't get out.'

'What am I supposed to do then? Even a cricket needs a crack to crawl through, so how am I supposed to get on without one?'

'I suggest you think it over and have a word with that clerk friend of yours. As for blocking every crack, I had the right to do it, because there's no mention of cracks in your lease.'

'Surely not? I can't believe it!'

'Well, that's how it is!'

'But look here, my dear fellow, it can't be true.'

'Instead of arguing, why don't you get down and have a look?'

'I think that's what I'd better do.'

The hapless Safronych thereupon clambered down from the roof, went into his house, fished out the lease he had signed with the former owner, put on his glasses, and started carefully to peruse the document. He read it through once, then again, and saw that he was indeed in a fix. The lease said nothing to the effect that any new owner of the site could not, if he so wished, nail up the gate into Safronych's premises and thus leave him with no means of entry or exit. But who would ever have thought of doing such a thing, apart from a German?

'Ugh, you swine, may a wolf eat you, like you've eaten me!' exclaimed the wretched Safronych; and he began banging on the fence that ran down the side of his premises and separated him from the house of a lady neighbour.

'My good woman,' he said to her, 'let me put a ladder up to your fence, so that I can get out into the street across your yard. Look what a fix that spiteful German has put me in,' he said, 'he's nailed me up, caught my legs in a fatal noose, he has, so I can't even get out to see my friend the clerk. Until I can get him in front of a judge, you won't let me and my little chicks starve, will you? Allow me to go in and out over your fence until the powers that be give me some protection against this bandit.'

His lady neighbour, who was of the tradesmen's class, took pity on him and let him over the fence.

'Don't you worry, my good man,' she said. 'As if I would stand in your way! You're a decent fellow, so put up your ladder, it won't cost me anything, and I'll fix up my own ladder for you on this side of the fence, so you can climb in and out as you please, just like crossing the highroad, until the authorities sort out your squabble with the German. They won't let him get away with his nasty tricks, even if he *is* a German.'

'That's what I reckon, ma'am; they won't let him.'

'Well, until they stop him, you hurry along and see Zhiga, he'll sort it all out for you.'

'That's exactly what I propose to do.'

'You run along then, dear. He'll pull some rabbit or other out of his hat, I'll be bound. In the meantime maybe, I can take a plank out of my fence for you.'

Safronych was reassured. A crack was opening up for him.

They set a ladder each side of the fence, and a line of communication, however inconvenient, was restored between Safronych's household and the outside world. His wife went off for water, while he hurried along to see Zhiga, who had drawn up his lease for him donkey's years ago. Sobbing, he gave vent to his resentment:

'See here,' he said, 'you kept on urging me not to give in to the German, and now look what's happened to me, and it's all your fault, and on your head be it that me and my little chicks will starve to death. So much for all your fine talk of "glory and prosperity"!'

The clerk merely smiled.

'You're a fool,' he said, 'you're a fool, my gentle brother, Vasily Safronych, and you're a coward into the bargain. No sooner has good fortune come to smile on you than you start hiding your face from it.'

'Just a moment,' replied Safronych. 'What's so fortunate about me and my family having to climb over somebody else's fence at all hours of day and night? I've never wanted that sort of good fortune! What's more, my children are still youngsters. What if I send one of them off on an errand: as likely as not he'll run a splinter into his belly, or fall down and break a leg. And what if, according to my conjugal rights, my wife gets with child every year, how easy will it be for her, do you think, to keep hopping over a fence? How are we supposed to get on in a state of siege like that? As for orders for work, what need I say? Leaving aside the question of how I'm supposed to drag out some walloping great boiler – what if I knock together a simple harrow or something? – I couldn't even find a way to get that out on to the road.'

The clerk was unrepentant.

'You're a fool, Vasily Safronych, that's what you are.'

'Why do you keep harping on about me being a fool? I can do without your rude names: what I need is some words of comfort.'

'Words of comfort? What do you need those for, when you have found favour with the Lord beyond your just deserts?'

'I haven't the foggiest idea what you're talking about.'

'You haven't the foggiest idea what I'm talking about precisely because you're a fool, such a fool that a man of my intelligence ought to be ashamed of himself for trying to make himself understood to an idiot like you. However, I'm answering you only because you have been blessed with such extravagant good fortune that my heart is glad when it contemplates the glorious life that awaits you. Now watch you don't forget what I have said, don't let the wind blow you off-course; don't let me down.'

'You're pulling my leg, you shameless fellow.'

'What's the matter with you, have you completely taken leave of your wits, that you can't understand what somebody tells you? This is not a joke. I tell you seriously: blessed art thou from this day forward – if you can only contrive not to drown in drink.'

Poor Vasily Safronych still didn't understand a thing, but Zhiga went on:

'Get off home now. Follow your highroad over the fence, but ask no favours of the German, and don't make peace with him. And whatever you do, don't let your neighbour make a hole in her fence for you. Just keep on going up and down the ladders, like I've told you; you can't have a better road than that.'

'Steady on, surely you can't mean we've got to go on clambering up and down?'

'And why not? You just keep on climbing, leave things as they are; it would be a sin to do anything to upset such a blessed state of affairs. Now, off home with you, and later in the day get out a carafe and some Kizlyar vodka,* because I shall be popping over that fence to celebrate by drinking the German's health with you.'

'You can come if you like, but you won't catch me drinking his health. I'd rather he came to my funeral feast and choked to death on a pancake.'

The clerk, who was in the greatest of good humour, comforted him:

'Brother, who knows what might happen? Such a splendid game has begun that I see no reason why even you shouldn't drink his health: and it could even be that he will come to your funeral and get a pancake stuck in his throat. You know what it says in the Scriptures: "He made a pit and digged it, and is fallen into the ditch which he made." And do you think he will not fall in?'

'Well, why should he? He's got all the advantages . . .'

'Ah, but then where is it written: "Neither let the mighty man glory in his might"? Oh faithless and perverse generation, how long shall I be with you? How long shall I suffer you? Learn of me, in what I put my trust: after all, it's fourteen years since I was sacked, and I still go on drinking vodka. Sometimes my heart is faint, and I am about to murmur against the Lord: then something will come my way, and again I will reach for the bottle and praise the Lord. Everything in this life, my friend, has its beginning and its end: only you, and you alone, have been granted unbroken bliss from this moment until the grave. Go and wait for me to come, and stretch your mouth a bit, the better to gape in wonder at what we will do to that German of yours. Pray only for one thing . . .'

'And what is that?'

'That he may outlive you.'

'Phoo!'

'Don't spit, I tell you, but pray – and in true faith, because things are going to get very hard for him from now on.'

XIV

Thus spake Zhiga, in naught but riddles.

Vasily Safronych trotted off back to the enclave which was his home, took the highroad over the fence, sent someone off by the same route to buy vodka for the clerk and sat down to await the latter's arrival in a state of confusion and despair, which, for all Zhiga's brave talk, he could not manage to shake off.

Zhiga for his part was not letting the grass grow under his feet. Tricked out in his rust-coloured uniform jacket, a cape round his shoulders and a hat, also of rusty hue, upon his head, he presented himself at Hugo Karlovich's door and requested to speak to him.

Pectoralis had just finished dinner and was sitting picking his teeth with a quill taken from a tiny beaded case; Klara Pavlovna had made it for him as a surprise in those blissful days when a radiantly happy Pectoralis had still not learned to fear his wife's little surprises, and his faith in her iron will was as yet unshaken.

Hearing that the clerk was at the door, Hugo Karlovich, who, as the master of his own affairs, had already begun to put on airs, kept him waiting; but when Zhiga let it be known that he came on important business, he said: 'Show him in.'

The clerk entered and bowed deeply to Pectoralis, which pleased the latter so much that he said: 'Do sit down, *bitte*.'

The clerk replied: 'Forgive me, Hugo Karlovich, how can I be seated in your presence? I have good Russian legs, of solid oak, and in your noble presence I can perfectly well stand.'

'Aha,' thought Pectoralis, 'this clerk, it would appear, holds me in proper respect and knows his place.' So he repeated: 'No, I insist, be seated, *bitte*.'

'Really, Hugo Karlovich, I prefer to stand in your presence. We Russians grow upright like trees, you know, and we're trained to do so from childhood. In particular, we're taught to be polite to foreign folk.'

'You're a sharp fellow, and no mistake!' laughed Pectoralis, and pushed his guest forcibly into an armchair.

Zhiga was left with no option other than to shift himself from the depths of the chair and perch respectfully on its edge.

'Now be so good as to announce your business. If you are a pauper, let me warn you that I give nothing to the poor: a poor man has only himself to blame.'

The clerk's jaw sagged: fixing Pectoralis with a stare of servile admiration, he replied:

'How truly you speak, sir. Every poor man is indeed responsible for his own plight. He who would seem to have been abandoned even by God is still himself to blame.'

'How so?'

'For not knowing what he should do about it, sir. I remember a case like that: we had a regiment quartered here, cavalry, or whatever you call them . . . on horses.'

'Cavalry.'

'That's right, cavalry. Well, one of their captains taught me all the philosophy there is to know.'

'I've never heard of a cavalry captain teaching philosophy.'

'Well this one did, sir. You see, something happened which gave him the chance to do it.'

'It could only happen by chance.'

'It was like this, sir. They were all mounted, having a smoke, and waiting for their commanding officer to arrive, when a poor German goes up to them and says: "*Seien Sie so gut*" and so on; you know, begging. The captain says: "Are you a German?" "Yes," he says, "a German." "Well then, what are you doing begging? Join the regiment and you can be like the general we're waiting for at this very moment." And he gave him nothing.'

'Nothing?'

'Nothing. And this fellow actually joined up and, they say, became a general, and booted that captain out.'

'Good man!'

'I agree; and that's why I always treat a German with respect, because God alone knows what may become of him.'

'This is a truly splendid fellow, a very fine fellow indeed,' ruminated Pectoralis, and he asked aloud:

'Well, it's a good story. Now what exactly is your business with me?'

'It's your business, sir.'

'Mine?'

'Just so, sir.'

'I don't know what business you're talking about.'

'No, sir, but you soon will.'

'With Safronych, you mean?'

'The same, sir.'

'He has no rights in the matter. His lease specifies a fence and that's what he's got.'

'He has, sir.'

'And it says nothing about a gate.'

'No sir, it doesn't, sir, not a word. But there's still going to be a fuss. He came to me and said: "I'm going to lodge a complaint."'

'Let him.'

'That's what I said. "Lodge a complaint, if you like," I said, "but there's nothing in your lease about a gate."'

'Just as I said!'

'Yes, sir, but he said . . . Will you permit me to report what he said?'

'Granted.'

'"I," he says, "even if I lose everything . . ."'

'He already has. The work he does is rubbish, his boilers all leak.'

'Leak, sir, yes, they do.'

'So as far as his work is concerned, it's finished.'

'Finished, sir, just as I told him: "It's all up with your factory, and nobody's going to help you; you can't bring things in through the gate or take them out." But he says: "I'll hop the twig before I give in to that German blighter."'

Pectoralis frowned and blushed.

'He really said that?'

'Would I dare to lie? That's exactly what he said, sir. He called you a blighter, and a something-something blighter into the bargain, *and* in front of a crowd of witnesses – well, you can reckon all the merchants heard him because all this conversation was conducted in the tavern on the gentlemen's side, where they were all taking tea.'

'What a scoundrel the man is!'

'He certainly is a scoundrel, sir. I tried to stop him: "Vasily Safronych," I says, "you want to be a bit more careful what you say about the German nation, because they often become pretty big fish over here." At that he went fairly white with rage and started laying it on really thick, so much so that the whole company present forgot all about their tea and their sugar-lumps, and began to listen, and with approval too.'

'What exactly did he say?'

'"That," he said, "is something new, but I'm a firm believer in the old ways. Now in the olden days," he went on, "it was laid down in writing by Tsar Aleksey Mikhaylovich that when the Germans first started coming to Muscovy, they, the something-something so-and-sos, shouldn't be allowed to live wherever they please, but should be confined to a separate district and assigned to the lowest social order."'*

'Hm! And was there in fact such a decree?'

'Certain books mention it as a fact.'

'It's a very bad decree.'

'I agree, not good at all, sir. Moreover, why should anyone recall it after so many years, and in the presence of a large crowd in a public place such as the gentlemen's side of a tavern, where all sorts of talk is heard, and men's minds naturally turn to political topics?'

'The rogue!'

'Of course, he behaved dishonourably, and I told him as much.'

'You told him?'

'Yes, sir, I did: and as a result of what I said, tempers were lost, and there was a good deal of bad language used, and then things got even worse.'

'How do you mean? You started to fight in the Russian way?'

'Exactly, sir. We fought the Russian way.'

'And did you give him a thrashing?'

'I thrashed him and he thrashed me: that's the way it goes in a proper Russian fight. Mind you, it was harder for him to win, of course, because, as you see, as a result of all the hard brainwork I do, my hair has all dropped out. What you see on top of my head is borrowed from the loan department, that is, from the reserves – I comb it up from the back. Whereas he is a shaggy sort.'

'He's shaggy all right, the scoundrel.'

'Indeed he is, sir. Now when I saw that peace was done with and war was breaking out, the first thing I did was to send back my own hair to the loan department, and grab him by the forelock.'

'Well done!'

'Well done indeed, sir – but he still gave me something to remember him by.'

'Never mind, that's nothing.'

'On the contrary, it's very painful, sir.'

'Never mind, I say. I'll pay the cost of repairs. Here, here's a rouble towards it straight away.'

'I thank you kindly. I knew I could rely on you; but that's not the end of the problem.'

'Then what is?'

'I'm afraid I've done something terribly rash.'

'Well?'

'After the first battle a short truce was struck, because we were dragged apart, and an argument began. As a result, well, I don't know how I could have been so mad, how I could have said what I did say about you.'

'About me?'

'Yes, sir. I took a bet on you, sir, that, well, as I put it – you go ahead and lodge your complaint, but you won't force Hugo Karlovich to act against his will, and you'll never make him open up those gates.'

'And the fool actually thought he would?'

'I make bold to say, sir, that he's sure of it, and the others are equally sure.'

'The others!'

'The whole lot of them, as one man.'

'We'll see about that, oh yes, we'll see about that!'

'It's going to be a real triumph for them, if you give way.'

'I? Give way?'

'Yes, sir.'

'Are you unaware that I am a man of iron will?'

'I have heard tell, sir: and it was relying on that fact that I decided to take such a gamble. You see, I laid a wager in the presence of the whole company, and I was so carried away I agreed to put down a hundred roubles on the spot.'

'Then put them down. You'll get two hundred back.'

'Yes, sir, but you see, I left the rest of them in the tavern, making as if I was running home to fetch the money, and came to see you instead. It's like this, Hugo Karlovich; apart from the odd two and a half roubles, I haven't got a kopeck at home.'

'That's a bad business! Why have you no money?'

'It's my own stupidity, sir. It's hard to live an honourable life in a country like ours.'

'That's true enough.'

'Indeed it is, sir. I'm a man who lives by his honour, and starves by it too.'

'Well, never mind. I'll give you the hundred roubles.'

'You're too kind: but they won't come to any harm. It all depends on you, after all.'

'Then they'll certainly come to no harm. When you collect your two hundred, keep a hundred for yourself and return my hundred to me.'

'I will, sir, have no fear.'

Pectoralis handed over a banknote to the clerk, who, as the door closed behind him, was so overcome with mirth that he was scarcely able to grope his way in the dark into the neighbouring garden, and thence over the fence to Safronych, to enjoy the latter's bottled token of gratitude.

'Rejoice and be glad, O Russian artlessness!' he said. 'Today I have caught the German on such a well sprung hook that he'll as soon wriggle off it as Satan will break his chains.'

'At least give me an idea what you're talking about,' Safronych insisted.

'I'll say no more than that he is caught, and caught by his own pride – which is a deadly noose.'

'That won't worry him!'

'Be silent, o thou of little faith! Do you not know that an angel, no less, rode that selfsame horse and tumbled to his doom, so why shouldn't our German come a cropper too?'

They drained their glasses and scribbled out an official complaint. The next morning Safronych, following his highroad over the fence, took it to the judge. Although he only half-believed the clerk's assertion that 'the outcome of the affair would be as favourable as it would be unexpected', he was nonetheless greatly reassured. He closed down his furnace, turned away orders, dismissed his workmen, and settled down to await whatever end the whole business might turn out to have. The clerk, however, experienced no agony of suspense: with great gusto he drank away in the town's taverns the hundred roubles out of which he had bilked Pectoralis. To add extra piquancy to the affair for all concerned – except, that is, Hugo Karlovich, for whom it added insult to injury – Zhiga went around boasting in his cups about how outrageously he had duped the German.

This all served to generate a mood of great expectancy in all the townsfolk, as they waited for the case of *Safronych v. Pectoralis* to come before the court. However, time went by: Pectoralis continued to puff himself up, like the frog that wanted to look like an ox;* Safronych, on the other hand, wore the front of all his clothes threadbare climbing over the fence, and losing heart, several times unbeknownst to Zhiga dispatched his wife and children to Pectoralis to ask for mercy.

Hugo was not to be moved.

'No,' he declared, 'I will come to see him at his invitation, but only to eat pancakes at his funeral. Until that day let the world see what is meant by my iron will.'

XV

At long last Safronych and Pectoralis received notification that their big day had arrived, and they both duly appeared at the courthouse.

Needless to say, the courtroom was packed. As I have said, the whole town was acquainted with every detail of the affair, including the revelations of the clerk Zhiga about how he had gulled Pectoralis. We, as former colleagues of Pectoralis, and our principals joined the rest of the throng who had come to listen and to watch. Everyone was keen to see what the court's decision would be and how the whole affair would end.

Pectoralis and Safronych both appeared without benefit of counsel. Pectoralis was apparently utterly convinced that he was in the right, and reckoned no one could make his case better than he could himself. Safronych was just plain unlucky. Zhiga had been keen to address the new court on his behalf and spent a long time preparing himself for it – indeed, he prepared himself so thoroughly that on the eve of the trial he toppled, drunk, from a bridge into a ditch and narrowly escaped dying the death of the 'Prince of poets'.* Safronych consequently sank even deeper into the dumps, while Pectoralis perked up considerably. He was about to parade the full might of his iron will, not before a single individual or a small family circle, but before the whole town. One had only to look at him to appreciate what significance he attached to this solemn moment. There could be no doubt, therefore, that he intended to make the most of it, to put on a display, to portray himself before his fellow citizens as a man of principle, a man worthy of respect, to cast a monument to himself in bronze, so to speak. It was, in a word, that 'moment', as our Russian officers say, upon which everything depends. Pectoralis knew that the bizarre tale of his wedding and marriage had provided material for many a joke, and had put the subject of his iron will on everybody's tongue. Such actual incidents as his sixty-day winter peregrination dressed only in an oilskin cape, his 'Russian fight' with Offenberg, and his naïve capitulation to the wiles of the drunken clerk, were supplemented by cock-and-bull stories of breathtaking improbability. And to be sure, Pectoralis recognized that fate had begun somehow to make cruel sport of him, and, as is always the case when things don't go your way, had started to undermine that which he held to be impregnable – his prudence, skill and powers of reason. Only a short time before, when he moved into the town, he had thought to astonish everyone by setting up a home rationally designed for easeful living; to this end he had installed a warm-air heating system. However, as a result of some crude miscalculation, the boiler in his cellar had turned red-hot and threatened to explode, while the house remained ice-cold. Pectoralis froze and obliged his wife to freeze with him, but would let no one through the door, lest they discover what was going on. He told everyone the house was beautifully warm. Rumours were rife in the town that he had gone mad and was trying to burn fresh air: those who spread this tale thought themselves frightfully witty. It was said that Pectoralis's chariot, on which he still rode about like a 'Mordvinian God', had run away with him out of mischief and disintegrated, just as he was fording a stream; that the armchair had leapt from its frame, and the horse had galloped home with the wheels, leaving Pectoralis sitting in his armchair in mid-stream, until the local chief of police, who happened to be passing, spotted him and shouted: 'What idiot has put an armchair in a stupid place like that?'

The idiot had proved to be Pectoralis.

The police chief had then allegedly rescued Pectoralis from the chair and carted him home to dry out in his chilly house. As for the armchair, many claimed to have seen it later, still lying in the stream, and the local peasantry had, so it was said, christened the spot 'the German ford'. It was difficult to ascertain how much of all this was truth and how much exaggeration. It appeared that Hugo Karlovich had indeed toppled off, spent some time sitting in the stream, and been brought home by the chief of police. The police chief retailed the incident himself, and the chariot of the God of the Mordvinians was not seen again. All these troubles – in accordance with the principle that it never rains but it pours – tumbled one after another upon Pectoralis's head, and made him something of a laughing-stock. This did nothing to enhance that fine reputation of his as a man of enterprise and determination – a reputation which curiously increased and decreased at one and the same time.

This wonderful Russia of ours, where things so rapidly reach a peak, and just as quickly roll down the other side, was beginning to affect even Pectoralis. Whereas yesterday, as far as his particular skill was concerned, his word had been law, today, after Zhiga had swindled him, he had lost his authority even in that respect.

The same chief of police who had pulled him from his perch in the stream and brought him home, invited him round to talk over some plans he had asked Pectoralis to draw for a new house.

'Look, my dear fellow,' he said, 'what I'd like is a façade about sixty feet wide, depending on the site, with six windows, and a balcony and door in the middle.'

'You can't have that many windows,' said Pectoralis.

'Why not?'

'It would spoil the proportions.'

'No, you don't understand; I'm building this house in the country.'

'Town or country, it makes no difference. I can't do it; it would spoil the proportions.'

'What are these proportions that we're supposed to have, in the country?'

'How do you mean? All buildings have proportions.'

'And I tell you, we don't. Just go ahead and put in the six windows.'

'And I say, you can't have six,' insisted Pectoralis. 'It's quite out of the question, the proportions don't allow it.'

The police chief looked hard at Pectoralis and emitted a whistle.

'I'm sorry to have to say this, Hugo Karlovich,' he said, 'but what can I do? It's obviously true what people say. All I can do is ask someone else to draw the plans.'

He thereupon went around telling everybody: 'Can you imagine how stupid that Hugo Karlovich is? I say to him: I want to build a house in the country with so many windows, and all he keeps saying is "The proportions don't allow it."'

'It can't be true!'

'It is; I swear it's true.'

'God, what a fool!'

'Just judge for yourselves. I say to him: Look, my dear chap, do see reason. I'm building this house on my own country estate: what have plans or proportions got to do with it? But no, try as I might, I couldn't talk the idiot round.'

'He certainly is an idiot.'

'He certainly is. I ask you – finding things like "proportions" on a landowner's estate. He's obviously crackers.'

'Obviously. Still, whose fault is it, eh? Ours!'

'Of course it's ours.'

'What were we doing singing his praises like we did?'

'Exactly.'

In brief, by this time Pectoralis's stock was fairly low; and if he'd appreciated what is meant by a 'bad patch' in general, and in Russia in particular, then he'd naturally have been wiser not to nail up Safronych's gate.

But Pectoralis didn't believe in 'bad patches', and didn't lose heart – of which commodity, as we shall see, he had considerably more than his past history might have led one to expect. He knew that it was vital not to lose heart, because, as Goethe said, 'to lose heart is to lose everything'. The Pectoralis who faced Safronych across the courtroom was the same unshakably determined Pectoralis whom I had encountered some time back in the chilly post-station at Vasilev Maidan. He had aged, of course, but the general appearance, the resolution, the unwavering self-assurance, the self-esteem – none of these had changed.

'Why no lawyer?' his acquaintances asked in a whisper.

'I have my own lawyer.'

'Who is that?'

'My iron will,' answered Pectoralis laconically. There was no time for further conversation. The moment of decision had arrived: the hearing had begun.

XVI

I so dislike describing courts of law and their proceedings that I shall decline to offer you any version of what went on at the hearing in terms of the people involved and what exactly they all did. I'll simply relate what happened.

Safronych fidgeted, as he stood respectfully in his brown frock-coat, the front of which was rather the worse for wear from fence-climbing, and, with a guileless nodding of the head and a vague waving of the arms, told his side of the story. Hugo stood, arms folded Napoleonically across his chest, either maintaining an imperturbable silence or answering questions in crisp, decisive monosyllables.

The facts of the case were simple and soon explained. Safronych's lease did not indeed make any mention of gates or rights of way. The tone of the examining judge indicated clearly that he felt sorry for Safronych, but that he could see no legal basis for taking his part. In this respect Safronych lost his case. Then suddenly the moon turned to reveal its previously unseen face. The judge produced documentary evidence indicating the material losses suffered by Safronych as a result of Pectoralis's high-handed action. The figures quoted were not inflated in any particular way; since the enforced closure of his factory, they were calculated to have been fifteen roubles a day.

The figure arrived at was clear, precise and indisputable. Safronych's loss would actually have amounted to that much *if* production at his factory had been what it should have been – which in fact it never had been, because of his sloppy, happy-go-lucky ways.

However, the court was concerned to establish only that daily loss which was claimed, and proved, to be possible.

'What do you have to say to that, Mr Pectoralis?' the judge enquired.

Pectoralis shrugged, smiled, and replied that it was no concern of his.

'But it is you who are causing him these losses.'

'That is no concern of mine,' answered Pectoralis.

'And you do not wish to settle your differences?'

'Never!'

'Why so?'

'Your honour,' answered Pectoralis, 'that is not possible. I am a man of iron will, everyone knows that. What I have once decided must be; it cannot be changed. I will not open the gate.'

'And that is your final word?'

'Yes, absolutely my final word.'

Pectoralis stood with jutting chin while the judge proceeded to write. It did not take him particularly long – but what he wrote was well written.

The court's decision represented a complete victory for Pectoralis's iron will, and at the same time dealt him a *coup de grâce*. To Safronych, just as Zhiga had predicted, it brought happiness beyond all expectation.

The verdict did not open the gate which Pectoralis had closed – it left untouched the German's right to indulge his iron will in this respect. On the other hand it bound Pectoralis to compensate Safronych for his losses to the tune of fifteen roubles a day.

Safronych was well content: but, to everyone's surprise, Pectoralis also pronounced his pleasure at the decision.

'I am well satisfied,' he affirmed, 'I said the gate would be nailed up, and that's how it will stay.'

'Yes, but it's going to cost you fifteen roubles a day.'

'Quite correct; but he has gained nothing.'

'He's gained fifteen roubles a day.'

'I am not referring to that.'

'Let's see, what does that come to? There are twenty-eight working days in a month . . .'

'Except for the feast of the Virgin of Kazan.'

'Yes, excepting that – that's two hundred and eighty, plus a hundred and forty – four hundred and twenty roubles a month in all. About five thousand a year. Good heavens, Hugo Karlovich, it's a funny sort of victory you've won, I'm blessed if it isn't. He would never have earned that much: he's made you his serf, that's what he's done.'

Hugo blinked, as the true cost of the affair dawned on him: but his iron will prevailed, and on the first of the month he lodged with the judge the sum required to ensure Safronych's ease and comfort and to compensate for his misfortune.

So it went on: on the first of the month, regular as clockwork, Safronych would hand in to the court the fifteen roubles monthly rent owed to Pectoralis, and bring back home over the fence the four hundred and twenty roubles which Pectoralis had handed over for him.

What a marvellous state of affairs! Life for Safronych took a spectacular turn for the better: he had never previously known, nor dreamed of knowing, such an easy, free and lucrative existence. He shut up his forges and his sheds and spent the day whistling softly to himself, drinking tea, sharing a bottle of vodka with the clerk Zhiga, then climbing back via his ladder for a quiet nap – in the meantime assuring all and sundry that 'I've got no grudge against the German; God sent him as a punishment for my simplicity. The only thing that worries me is that he might die before I do. God forbid that should happen; he's promised to come and eat pancakes at my funeral, and he's a man of his word. When the time comes, wife, you make sure he has a good plateful, and in the meantime may God preserve him for many a year yet to work for me.'

And being a man of a genuinely forgiving nature, Safronych always displayed the utmost affability towards Hugo Karlovich; when he met him in the street, he would already at some distance from him doff his hat, bow, and yell:

'Good day to you, Hugo Karlovich, my dear sir! Good day to you, benefactor!'

Hugo did not appreciate this artless cordiality; he took it as an insult.

'Out of my way, muzhik,' he would reply angrily, 'follow the path I've laid for you, over the fence.'

To which the good-natured Safronych would respond:

'My dear fellow, why lose your temper? Why get angry? If I have to climb the fence, I'll climb the fence – entirely as you wish – but I hold you in the greatest respect and I've no desire to insult you.'

'You just try insulting me!'

'I wouldn't dare, your honour, I wouldn't dare – and I've no reason to either. On the contrary, my family and I, we pray for you night and morning.'

'I can do without your prayers.'

'Ah, but we can't. You see, you're our benefactor, and we pray that God will preserve you. I keep telling the children: don't you forget to pray, my little chicks – I say – that he, our benefactor, should live a hundred years at least – and then crawl on all fours for another twenty.'

'What's all this about "all fours"?' Pectoralis pondered. '"Live a hundred years and crawl for twenty . . . on all fours." This "all fours" – is that a nice or nasty thing to say?'

He decided to seek enlightenment on this point, and discovered that it was much nastier than nice. Henceforth, this particular greeting became a new form of torment for him. Safronych, of course, did not desist, but kept yelling:

'Long life and good health to you, and may you crawl on all fours as well!'

Safronych's family, having lost their lawsuit, remained restricted to the fence as a means of communication with the outside world, but thanks to the indemnity extracted from Pectoralis, were better off than they had ever been, and, just as Zhiga had predicted, enjoyed a life of tranquillity and ease. On the other hand, for Pectoralis, who had won, things were turning out very badly indeed.

The indemnity he had to pay, month in, month out, was so burdensome that it not only swallowed all his profits, but threatened him with complete and utter ruin.

True, he put a brave face on things and was never heard to complain. In fact, he wore the cheerful air of a man who has stood up for his rights in public and won the public's respect. Nonetheless, one could already discern something rather sham in this cheerful manner. And after all, there was no way this obstinate man could fail to see where it was all leading, and he could hardly be expected to be looking forward with a light heart to the comical yet hopeless outcome of the affair. The situation was quite simple: no matter how hard he worked or how much he earned, it was all for the benefit of Safronych. His profits in the first year could not have exceeded five or six thousand, and out of that sum nothing could have remained for investment in the business or even for his own living expenses. His business had hardly been set up, therefore, before it had begun to go downhill, and its painful end was already in sight. Pectoralis's willpower was great, but his capital was too small to withstand such caprices on the part of fate. The money he had accumulated in Russia strove to return whence it had come, to flow back into the stream from which it had been drawn. Pectoralis was undergoing a terrible test, and had clearly resolved to perish rather than submit. God alone knows how it would all have ended, had not fate intervened to prepare a totally unforeseen dénouement.

XVII

A year passed, then a second, during which the situation I have described remained unchanged. Pectoralis continued to shell out and sink into poverty; Safronych went on drinking, and having finally gone completely to the dogs, took to wandering the streets like a vagabond. Such a situation was clearly not doing much good to either party. There was one party, however, who was determined to set the whole affair on a more rational footing. This was Marya Matveyevna, Safronych's wife, who was cut from the same rough cloth as her husband, but, unlike her husband, had the foresight to realize: 'Now if we strip the German of his last kopeck, what's going to happen then?'

This observation was based on good sound sense, and had important consequences. Marya Matveyevna had noted – and it would have been hard to overlook the fact – that by the end of the second year Pectoralis's factory was standing idle and Hugo himself was walking about in bitterly frosty weather without a fur coat, wearing just an old threadbare jacket, from which, purely for the sake of appearances, dangled a pince-nez. He had sacrificed not only all his property, but his reputation too – except, that is, for the reputation of a clown which he had earned by the exercise of his iron will. This new reputation, it has to be said, was of little practical value.

At this time another catastrophe befell him: he was abandoned by his darling spouse, and abandoned, what's more, in the most shameless and treacherous manner, for she took with her everything she could lay her hands on. To add to his misery, everyone took Klara Pavlovna's part, saying she had every reason to run away, because Pectoralis had installed a funny sort of furnace in his house, which heated the passageways but left the rooms ice-cold, and secondly because he was an altogether odd character, the sort of viperous fellow no one could possibly be expected to live with: he would get some weird notion in his head, then insist that everything be done accordingly. People even confessed themselves surprised that his wife hadn't left him earlier and robbed him when his affairs were in somewhat better shape and he hadn't yet handed everything over to pay Safronych.

Poor Hugo thus ended up being stripped clean, and held entirely responsible into the bargain: moreover, you couldn't say he didn't deserve to take some of the blame. Of course, it was wrong to rob him, but he must really have been an impossible man to live with, and that's why he ended up alone in the world. He was already in queer street too, but he still wouldn't give in and abandon his iron will. Safronych, as I've said, was no better off: he spent all his time in taverns and pot-houses, and continued to taunt the German, every time he met him, by wishing him a hundred years of health and twenty more on all fours.

If only *that* at least had not been so; if only Pectoralis had been spared this humiliation and abuse, he would have found things easier to bear.

So finally – largely just to avoid stalemate, you might think – Pectoralis lodged a complaint against Safronych, seeking retribution for the 'all fours', on which, in the view of Pectoralis, no German would ever have cause to crawl.

'It is he who is frequently to be seen on all fours, crawling out of taverns,' declared Pectoralis, pointing at Safronych. But fortune was as blind in favouring Safronych as she was stubborn in pursuing Pectoralis – and the judge firstly declined to share Pectoralis's view of the phrase 'all fours', and could see no reason why a German too should not sometimes crawl on them; secondly, examining the phrase in the context in which it was used, he found that Safronych's expressed wish that Pectoralis might crawl on all fours after living to a hundred represented an attitude of the utmost benevolence, expressing as it did the hope that Pectoralis would enjoy remarkable longevity: on the other hand the German's use of the same term to describe Safronych's mode of exit from taverns was defamatory, for which Hugo should be liable to the appropriate financial penalty.

Hugo couldn't believe his ears and considered it all to be an

appalling shambles and an outrageous Russian injustice. All the
same, when the overjoyed Safronych duly demanded damages,
Pectoralis was ordered to pay him ten roubles, which left him
quite distraught. His last kopecks had to be handed over to
compensate Safronych for the 'all fours' insult. Having paid up,
he felt there was nothing left to do but curse the day he was born,
and perish together with his iron will. And that, no doubt, is
what he would have done, had he not been bound by his
resolution to outlive his enemy and eat pancakes at his funeral.
That was a promise he simply had to keep!

He found himself in a situation somewhat akin to that of
Hamlet, torn between two desires and two resolutions – and, in
his present rather battered state, could not decide 'whether 'tis
nobler in the mind' – to exercise his will by committing suicide
or, by applying that same will, to drag out his thoroughly
miserable existence.

The ten roubles damages he had paid to Safronych for
defamation of character were his last: he had nothing to cover the
next month's indemnity payment.

'Ah well,' he said to himself, 'they'll come to my house and see
I have nothing left . . . *I have nothing left*, and I have had nothing
to eat today, and tomorrow . . . tomorrow also I shall starve, and
the day after as well – and then I shall die. Yes, I shall die, but my
will shall remain of iron.'

Meanwhile, as Pectoralis, who really was in a sorry plight, was
living through his most desperate hour, fate was preparing
another sudden crisis, which I am at a loss to know how to
describe – whether as lucky or unlucky for him. The fact is that
precisely at this moment something important was happening in
Safronych's life, something which was to turn the whole situation
topsy-turvy and write the most improbable finale to the story of
the battle between these two heroes.

XVIII

It has to be said that while Pectoralis and Safronych were engaged in litigation, and the former was gradually bankrupting himself by making over his total assets to the latter in regular fixed amounts, this latter, despite having become an habitual drunkard, was better placed than his rival. This he owed to his wife, who had not abandoned him, as Klara had abandoned Pectoralis. On the contrary, Marya Matveyevna had taken her sottish husband in hand. She took to paying the rent herself, and at the same time confiscating the monthly payments made by Pectoralis to Safronych. To avoid quarrelling with her befuddled muzhik and to ensure his compliance, she did not make life too hard for him and handed over fifty kopecks a day, which he retained the right to squander as he pleased. It all went one way, of course. Having drunk away his fifty kopecks during the day, Safronych would return home in the evening by way of the now familiar ladder over the fence. No degree of inebriation could divert him from this route. God, who, according to popular belief, protects infants and drunkards, maintained his merciful watch over Safronych, whether in darkness, rain, snow or black ice. Safronych never failed to climb the ladder safely, reach the top of the fence, and topple safely down the other side, where a heap of straw had been thrown precisely to meet this eventuality. It was his intention to go on this way until the very last day of those hundred and twenty years of living and crawling which he had promised Pectoralis. He never dreamed that Pectoralis's funds might dry up. Who had ever heard of a German in Russia running short of cash? It might happen to any other man easily enough, but a German – he would always have enough.

Safronych's wife, however, in her womanly simplicity, unswayed by prejudice, chose to think otherwise, and by laying her hands on all the money exacted from Pectoralis by her husband, had put together a small amount of capital. In order to avoid further clambering over fences, she used this money to buy a little house, a nice little house, clean, bright, on a high foundation, with a mezzanine and a tall, steeply pitched roof – in a word, a dinky little house, and, what was more, situated right next door to the old place, where their life had been disrupted by that man of iron, Hugo Pectoralis.

She made the purchase precisely at the time when Pectoralis was suing Safronych for 'all fours'; and on the day the former iron-founder won his unexpected victory over the German and received his ten roubles damages, the whole Safronych household were moving into their new quarters and settling down to enjoy the sort of comfortable life they had not known for a long time.

Safronych himself took no part in all this; the family, which had long since ceased to rely on him for anything, did not expect him to help and organized the whole business exactly as it pleased and as best it knew how.

Safronych meanwhile, having received what was for him the considerable sum of ten roubles, said nothing about it to his wife and, having slipped away undetected to the tavern, launched himself on a prodigious binge.

The first three days and nights which his family spent in their new home, he spent roaming from tavern to tavern, pot-house to pot-house, carousing in the company of good friends, and wishing the German a hundred years of good health and as long again on all fours. In charitable mood, he gladly granted Pectoralis this increment, and loudly lamented:

'I'm a stupid man, a very stupid man. How right Zhiga was – God rest his soul! – when he said that I was stupid, and that this German had been sent to me as manna from heaven. And for what? "What is man, that thou art mindful of him? Or the son of man, that thou visitest him?" Where is that written?'

'In the Scriptures.'

'Yes, exactly – in Holy Scripture. And how often do we remember what is written there? Oh, how we forget, how completely we forget!'

'It is a weakness.'

'A weakness it is, to be sure. I am a worm, not a man, a reproach of men. Yet if God so wishes, he will protect even the worm, he will take care of you better than you could ask, better than you could dream of. If you are weak, he will send you a German, that you may live off his wits.'

'Just watch out for one thing,' his companions warned him. 'Be careful your German doesn't finally crack and open the gate.'

The besotted Safronych had no such fears.

'Open the gate?' he replied. 'He'll never do that, he's got his nation's reputation to think about. They've got this rule, you see, that if you say you'll do something, you do it.'

'My God, the swine!'

'Yes, that's the way it is with them. He said it, didn't he, clear as you like, in the court? "I've got an iron will," he said. Now how can he hope to get along with that on his back? Things are bad enough for him as it is.'

'Yes, he's in a bad way.'

'I wouldn't wish any man to be cumbered with a will like that, and particularly a Russian – it would be the end of him.'

'It would. It would finish him off.'

'Let's have another drink. Why talk about things like this, when it's already nearly evening? All I can say is I hope he lives a hundred years and outlives me.'

'Aye, brother, let's hope he does.'

'That's what I say too – because at least he'll draw some comfort from that.'

'How's that?'

'Well, he'll be able to come and eat his pancakes!'

'You've got a kind heart, Safronych!'

'Yes, I have, I have: you know, I would like him to live longer than me . . . but only by a tiny, tiny bit.'

'Yes, just a touch.'

'That's right, that's right . . . just up to this mark on my glass.'

'That will do nicely.'

'Yes, just up to this little mark.'

Measuring off the quantity in question, the friends drank; they then proceeded to drink the health of all and sundry; and finally, after drinking to the memory of their benefactor, the clerk Zhiga, who had heaped all these blessings upon them, they struck up in loud, tuneless voices a lament for the dead. It was at this point that there occurred that strange beginning of the end, which has never been explained to this day.

The drunkards had scarcely completed their lament, when there was a sudden loud banging on the window which gave on to the yard, and from the darkness a hideous face peered in. The innkeeper, taking fright, instantly blew out the light and shoved his guests without ceremony out into the dark street. The companions found themselves up to their knees in mud, and rapidly lost contact with each other in the thick, slimy autumn fog. Safronych foundered in the fog like a fly in lather, and lost all sense of what was going on.

Barely capable of standing upright, he tried for some time to stuff into his pocket an unopened bottle of vodka which he had grabbed as he was being hustled out. He then made as if to call somebody, but his tongue, which had known no rest for three days, was suddenly so struck by fatigue, so paralysed, that he could not utter a sound. As if that were not bad enough, his legs turned out to be in no better shape than his tongue, and were as reluctant to walk as his tongue was to talk. In fact he was no good for anything at all: his eyes could not see, his ears could not hear, and he had an overwhelming urge to sleep. 'Oh no you don't, damn you! You won't catch me that way!' he thought to himself. 'That's how Zhiga went to sleep, and he didn't wake up again:

but I don't want to die just yet, and let that German outlive me by years. I don't mind if he outlives me, as long as it's only by a little bit.'

That raised his spirits: he took a few paces more and, sensing that the mud was now higher than his knees, once more came to a halt. 'Good grief, if you're not careful, you could drown here, as easily as in England,' he kept saying to himself. 'But where the devil am I, and where's my house? Eh? Where, for God's sake, is my house? Where's my ladder?'

'The devil has swallowed it with a glass of kvass.'

'Who is that saying the devil has swallowed my house with a glass of kvass? Eh? Come on out! If you're a decent fellow, I'll treat you to some vodka. If you're not, we'll have a fight the Russian way.'

'That suits me!' said a voice from the fog, and at that instant Safronych received a blow on the ear which knocked him clean off his feet into the mire.

'Hey, that's enough of that,' he thought, 'my memory's gone completely, I haven't a clue what's going on. And where have all those friends of mine got to? The rotten boozers! It's true what they say – never go drinking with drunkards. I'll never go drinking with drunkards again, that's for sure. What? Who's that keeps talking to me? Listen here, tell me, will you, what do you want from me? You won't find anything, brother: I've hidden the bottle underneath me. Ouch! stop, stop! Why grab me by the hair like that? It hurts. It's not doing me any good at all. Now he's going for my ears again – well, at least that'll help bring my memory back; but it hurts! Maybe I'd better get back on my feet.'

Thereupon, only half-willingly, and not really knowing what he wanted to do, he got to his feet and began to walk – or so it seemed. He couldn't be completely sure. The way it seemed to him, either he was walking forward, or the ground was simply receding beneath his feet. But something was happening for sure, someone was leading him, holding him up, and saying nothing.

Only once whoever it was said: 'Ah, so that's who you are!', and led him further.

'What's all this? Who is this leading me? What if it's the devil? There's something amiss, that's for certain. Still, as long as he takes me to my ladder, I'll find my own way from there.'

Eventually Safronych's guide brought him to the foot of a ladder and said: 'Up you go, and hold on tight to the rail.'

The walk had restored Safronych's power of speech, and he replied: 'Just a moment, brother, just a moment. I know my own business better than you. My ladder's got no rail.'

His guide wasted no time talking: instead, grabbing hold of Safronych, he began beating him around the ears again, as though braking birch-bark.

'Now do you remember it?' he said.

'Well,' thought Safronych, 'perhaps I'd better say I do', and he set off up the ladder.

He climbed and climbed, but there seemed no end to it.

'Strike me down if this is my house!' he thought.

The higher he climbed, the more clearly he recalled how he used to climb his own ladder, and how, with every rung, the light would increase, until the stars, the moon and the azure canopy of the sky opened up above him. But now, while it was true that the weather was foul, very strange things indeed were happening: the higher he climbed, the darker it became. Why could he not see his hand in front of his face? Why was it so dark all around? Why did he feel squeezed in from every side? And why the choking smell of soot and ash? And still there was no end of it, no promised fence-top, from which Safronych should long since have taken his downward plunge: instead, his path lay ever upwards. Then suddenly there was a terrible stunning blow on the crown of his head, causing not sparks, but whole broad shafts of light to pour from his eyes, and to illuminate . . . who do you think? – none other than the clerk Zhiga!

Pray do not assume that Safronych was dreaming or something of that kind. No, everything happened exactly as I have described it. Safronych climbed an endless ladder, came face to face with Zhiga, whom he recognized in the light, and said:

'Well, if it be God's will, good day to you.'

Zhiga, sitting on a seat of stone, nodded and replied:

'Greetings. I'm glad you've called: we've been drawing rations for you for ages.'

'So that's where I am . . . My word, it's dark here in hell. Still, there's nothing to be done about it; I suppose this is where I was bound to end up.'

Safronych sat down, pulled out the bottle, took as long a swig as he could manage, and passed it to Zhiga.

XIX

While these strange adventures were happening to the disorientated and drunken Safronych, leaving him sitting in the company of the late Zhiga on some incomprehensible devilish peak, which he took for the very pit of hell, his family were spending a very anxious night in their new house.

Despite having exhausted themselves moving all their goods and chattels and settling into their new home, they found their sleep constantly interrupted by the most curious noise, which began before midnight and went on practically until morning. To start with, Safronych's wife and the rest of the household heard someone walking about in the attic directly above their heads – at first, a quiet scuffling, like a hedgehog, then what seemed like angry sounds: something being picked up and put down, something being hurled about, in brief, an awful racket which made it impossible to get any rest. One or two of them thought they detected the sound of talking, a sort of low ringing noise, and a generally indecipherable rumbling. Those who woke first listened anxiously to all this din, woke up the others, crossed themselves and decided with one accord that the disturbance above their heads was nothing more or less than the mischief of some evil spirit, which, as every Orthodox believer knows, is wont to sneak into a new house before the occupants arrive and take up residence, preferably somewhere up at the top, such as in a hayloft or attic, that is, generally speaking, in those parts of the house where no icons hang.

Obviously, this was precisely what had happened to the good Safronych family – a devil hd popped into their new house before they had moved in. There could be no other explanation, because the first thing Marya Matveyevna had done when she entered the house was personally to chalk a cross on every door, and in taking these precautions she had not overlooked either the bathroom door or the one leading to the attic. It being thus obvious that the evil spirit had no means of entry, it was equally obvious that it had sneaked in beforehand.

And yet, as it turned out, that might not have been the explanation. The troubled night passed and morning approached. The family's fears subsided, and Marya Matveyevna, leaving the room first, saw that the door at the foot of the attic stairs had been flung open, concealing the chalk cross which she had marked with her own pious hand. Thus this entrance had been completely unprotected against the devil.

Marya Matveyevna, upon discovering this lapse, immediately conducted an enquiry to discover who was the last person to go up into the attic on the previous day.

After a lengthy investigation and a good deal of squabbling among the smaller members of the household, suspicion, and then fairly strong proof, pointed to one of the younger daughters, the barefooted Fenka, who had been born with a harelip and consequently was nobody's favourite. If anyone still treated her with any sympathy, it was her drunken father, who could not see that the child herself was much to blame for having been born with a harelip, and who did not therefore curse and beat her. The girl lived, as they say, like a prisoner in her own family: half-starved, charged with the dirtiest chores, she slept on the floor, went barefoot, without a warm jacket, dressed in rags and tatters. The evidence clearly indicated that on the previous evening she had gone up alone, carrying a lantern, to stuff rags into the flue,* and probably, being nervous, had rushed back downstairs and forgotten to shut the door behind her. The door had thus been left with its chalked cross, its defence against the arch-foe, facing the wall. The arch-foe, naturally, had then taken his chance, nipped up to the attic, and taken great delight in keeping a good Christian family awake all night. Of course, he doubtless also had plenty on his plate, since he too was settling into new quarters: but Marya Matveyevna took a rather selfish view of that, making no allowances at all for other folks' problems. She sought to put the matter right by calling the guilty party to account, and in doing so ignoring all notions of leniency or justice. Having run the harelipped Fenka to earth behind the stove, she dragged her by the hair to the door, and there set about giving her a good shaking and pronouncing sentence as follows:

'I'll stop the devil following in your tracks, you see if I don't. I'm going to shut this door with your head.'

She thereupon, as promised, banged the girl's forehead against the door hard enough to drop the catch. Instantly the devil went berserk again, this time with sudden and terrifying violence. Hardly had the child's pitiful squeal of pain faded into silence, when immediately above the heads of the assembled household something began whirling and running about, and a brick was hurled with great force against the other side of the door.

This was going too far. Marya Matveyevna had been brought up on all the old authentic tales of devils and the various sorts of mischief they get up to in Christian houses, and she had heard of their habit of throwing about anything that came to hand: but, to be honest, she had always taken this for idle talk. That a devil should have the cheek to run amok and start hurling stones at

people, and in broad daylight to boot – that she wasn't prepared
for; so it isn't surprising that she dropped her arms to her sides in
astonishment, thus releasing the girl, who shot out into the yard
and began rushing in and out of the outbuildings in search of
refuge. No sooner had the rest also dashed out into the yard in
pursuit of her – for they still held her responsible for the whole
rumpus – than the devil went on the rampage yet again. One
must assume that his arms had fully materialized, because whole
bricks and chunks of masonry were raining down on the hunters
with such savagery and violence that they all took fear for their
lives and, chanting 'the power of the cross be with us', vanished
as if by magic into an open hen-coop and hid in the safest spot,
beneath the perch.

Here, to be sure, they were very well placed, in that the devil
could not, of course, touch them, because it is from the perch that
the cock crows at midnight in response to particular mysterious
commands, regarding which the devil knows something or other
which he has good reason to fear. Still, you couldn't stay hidden
under a perch for ever: at dusk the chickens would arrive, and the
position immediately beneath the grating on which they perched
would become unsafe in quite a different respect.

XX

Now, as soon as the people who had taken refuge in the hen-coop
recovered from the panic which had gripped them, they did what
most superstitious cowards do: from terror they began to shift to
a sort of scepticism. The first to make a move was the hired
woman Marfutka, a lively wench, who didn't fancy sitting still
for long in a hen-coop: she was followed by the labourer Yegorka,
a lame but sprightly lad with ginger hair, who never missed a
chance to exchange whispers with Marfutka. On this occasion too
they resorted to this favourite occupation, and after whispering a
bit, came, you might say, to some very startling conclusions.

Their minds, which had long since worked in harmony, penetrated to the very heart of the matter and were inclined to suspect that there was perhaps an altogether different sort of devilry afoot here.

It struck them that all the nocturnal hullabaloo and the present barrage of stones was the work not of the devil, but of some unscrupulous rogue: and that rogue, in their view, could most likely – and even without question – be identified as the German, Pectoralis.

Out of sheer malice and envy the villain must have stolen into the house, and had now started throwing things at them.

Marya Matveyevna, hearing this theory, threw up her hands in astonishment, so improbable did it seem. A raiding party was promptly despatched from the hen-coop to get to the root of the matter and take all necessary steps to cut off the malefactor's line of retreat.

The labourer Yegorka and Marfutka, hand in hand, dashed from the hen-coop, removed the padlock from the barn door, and with it made fast the door to the attic: then, after pausing in the passageway to exchange a few private whispers, went their separate ways. Yegorka ran to tell the neighbours what had happened and invite their help in smoking out the German from his lair in the attic, while Marfutka took up position by the door with a pair of fire-tongs in order to belabour Pectoralis, should he by some Germanic wile manage to come through it. The German, however, stayed quiet as a mouse, and Marfutka caught no glimpse of him. The only action came from Yegorka, who nipped smartly out through the side gate and set off full-tilt for the market place: turning the corner, he came face to face with Hugo Karlovich. He was so dumbfounded that for a second he didn't know what to do: then he grabbed the German by the collar and yelled for help. Pectoralis, taken aback, whacked Safronych's labourer across the pate with his rolled umbrella and knocked him sideways into a puddle. The curious amalgam of

sensations he experienced as he received this soft but swingeing
blow with an umbrella and then went sailing into the mire so
astonished Yegorka that he could only sit in the puddle and bawl:

'Begone, devil, begone!'

All the suspicions inspired in him by Marfutka were instan-
taneously dissipated. However simple the poor lad was, he
couldn't fail to see that unless the German had managed to get
through a door secured with the padlock from the barn, then one
had to assume that the person running riot up in the attic was not
he, but someone else entirely. At this point, Yegorka's less than
nimble brain, lacking Marfutka's encouragement, inclined again
towards suspecting the devil of being responsible for the uproar
in the house. It was precisely in that light that he presented the
affair to the crowd in the market place. The crowd took great
pleasure in the news and rushed *en masse* to Marya Matveyevna's
house, where, judging by what Yegorka had said, things were
happening that were most unusual, and yet, as any spiritualist
would confirm, entirely within the bounds of possibility – the
sort of things that in the view of many learned men of our day
reveal how close to us the beings of the unseen world actually are.

XXI

By evening the whole town had been round to Marya Matveyevna's and everyone had heard, several times retold, the tale of the
supernatural goings-on of the preceding night and morning. Even
some representative of the police turned up, but nobody would
tell him anything, lest – which God forbid – things should end up
in a worse mess than ever. The local teacher of mathematics also
called round. He was a correspondent of a learned society, and
asked to be given the bricks that the demon or devil had hurled,
so that he could send them off to Petersburg.

Marya Matveyevna refused this request point-blank, lest evil
consequences ensue: but the astute Marfutka nipped out to the

bath-house, pulled out one of the bricks supporting the bench by the stove and brought it back.

The teacher seized this material evidence and bore it off to the local chemist: the two of them spent a long time examining it, sniffing it, licking it, pouring some acid or other on it, until in unison they pronounced:

'It's a brick.'

'Yes, I think we can safely claim it's a brick.'

'I agree,' answered the chemist.

'Perhaps it's not worth sending it off after all?'

'I would agree with that,' answered the chemist.

But more pious folk, who are less concerned with scientific analyses and suchlike, spent their time much more profitably and derived a good deal more interest from the affair. Some of them, who were endowed with a particularly high degree of sensitivity and patience, sat on in the Safronych house until they too were privileged to detect, coming through the door to the attic, a sound as of someone sighing and quietly treading about, like a soul undergoing the torments of hell. True, there were a few bold spirits among this company too; thus, one of them was ready to vote for taking a peek into the attic through the skylight, but such audacity struck everybody present as such audacity that the idea was promptly and unanimously rejected. This decision took account also of the fact that the proposed venture would be highly risky, if only because it wasn't so long since bricks had been flung out of the skylight in question, and the barrage might well be renewed. Anyone attempting such observation might easily, therefore, be considerably incommoded.

Marya Matveyevna, as a woman, had recourse to that patented womanly device – complaining.

'Of course,' she said, 'if I only had the sort of husband other folk are blessed with, that is, a man who's master in his own house, it would be his job to climb up and see what's going on.

But my husband is off on a spree, it's five days already since he's
been home.'

'Quite right,' her lady neighbours agreed, 'even the devil won't
strike a man in his own house.'

'I wouldn't be too sure of that.'

'All right, but if a man does get struck by the devil, that's his
look-out.'

There was still no sign of Safronych, and nobody had any idea
where to look for him, or which tavern to start with. He could
have gone off drinking in some village miles away.

'There's no point in worrying about him, Marya Matveyevna,
my love,' they all pronounced, 'what you should be thinking
about is how best to deal with Old Nick.'

'Yes, but tell me if you please, my dear friends, what *do* I do?'

'There's only one thing you can do, my pet: either call for Foka
the cobbler to coax the demon out, or use holy water.'

'It's ridiculous to think of using Foka. God knows what's
happening here as it is, and Foka is one of the devil's breed
himself.'

'Exactly. Who ever heard of one devil chasing out another?'

'Well, if that's the way you think, then you'll just have to use
holy water.'

'I'm agreeable to that: I even thought of it myself last night, but
then turned over and forgot. Let me just get the place tidied up,
then I'll bake some pies and bring an icon from the church, and
then let them come and purify the house with water. It's a
nuisance though that Safronych isn't at home.'

'Well, it's no good waiting for him!'

'Of course not. Still, it would be nicer, and he does so like the
service, the dear man. He always made a point of carrying the
bowl himself and walking in front of the priest through all the
rooms and chanting all the prayers. How we can do it without
him I don't know. And I can't think who we should ask to take
the service.'

'Ask for the archpriest, he's an older man; the devil's more likely to be frightened of him.'

'He's a fine one to choose. He smokes like a chimney. No, I'm not having him, with a cigarette forever stuck in his mouth. I'd rather ask Father Flavian.'

'Yes, he'd be all right too.'

'He's a bit on the stout side, mind you.'

'Yes, he's a nice soft plump fellow, and very kind: it's not that long since he blessed the Ilins' crushing mill, and he made a very good job of it. Mind you, you do have to take care that he sprinkles the holy water in all the nooks and crannies: he is a bit tubby, when all's said and done, and if there's anywhere he can't get into, he just sprinkles it as best he can, from a distance – and that's no good.'

'We'll have to watch out for that.'

'Yes, provided there's someone who knows what's what to keep an eye on him, it'll be all right.'

'Obviously, you have to make sure he sprinkles crosswise, and with the right words. But wait a minute: Father Flavian, the size he is, he's never going to get through that door to the attic.'

'That's true; he'll never make it.'

'You mean we'll have to widen it? That would cost a fortune.'

'It would.'

'I'll tell you what. Why not let Father Flavian bless the water, but have Deacon Savva get up into the attic to sprinkle it? I should ask him, if I were you; he's so skinny, he could get anywhere. It's the best plan; otherwise Father Flavian with that belly of his will quite likely fall down the stairs and kill himself.'

'God save us from such a sin, and preserve the old man too, good obliging fellow that he is! I was once suffering something terrible in labour, and I sent out to ask the archpriest to open the holy gates* for me, but he flatly refused.'

'You didn't give him enough, that's obvious.'

'I sent him a rouble; but Father Flavian, the lovely man, he flung them wide open for fifty kopecks.'

'Yes, he's a virtuous old man; let's get him to stay downstairs here and keep repeating the prayers, while Deacon Savva goes up by himself with the water and the *kropilo*:* it won't matter to him if any evil befalls him: his wife goes mad at least once a month, so I should think he's been finding life a bit of a burden for some time.'

'Yes, he's all right, he'll go; he does as the priest tells him. He'll go anywhere you like and make a good job of sprinkling. All you have to watch is that he doesn't hurry or skimp it: make sure he sprinkles crosswise.'

'I'll keep an eye on him, all right,' replied Marya Matveyevna. 'If God grants me the courage, I might even go up with him. I don't care, as long as it does the trick.'

'Heavens, what next? Provided it's all done properly, how can it fail to do the trick? Just get it done as soon as you can, and with as much ceremony as possible.'

'However could it be done with more ceremony than what I have in mind, my loves?' replied Marya Matveyevna. 'I'll get Marfutka to make the dough for the pies right away, and I'll send Yegorka to Father Flavian to ask him to come round tomorrow straight after early service.'

'That will do splendidly, Marya Matveyevna.'

'Well, why put things off, I say. Do you think I enjoy living under the same roof as the devil, and waiting for the wretch to start chucking things about? If I only had some pies ready, I'd ask the priest round this very day.'

'You're quite right, Marya Matveyevna, you can't do anything without the pies. The priests always have to have something like that. When you think about it, Father Flavian is as soft as a ball of cotton himself and he does like doughy things.'

Thus endorsing Marya Matveyevna's plans, her advisers further recommended that the unfortunate family should somehow put up with the unpleasantness of another day and night, that meanwhile the preparation of the pies should be put in hand, and

Yegorka should be sent off to Father Flavian with a request that he come straight from morning service to Marya Matveyevna's, bringing Deacon Savva with him, to sanctify the water in the house, exorcize the devil, and then sample a nice fresh pie.

Father Flavian was a gouty old man in a greasy *kamilavka*,* as plump as a dumpling and as soft as a feather mattress, with a bushy white beard and a massive paunch. After listening to Yegorka's account of the devil's deeds, and the request that he should come and drive it out, he replied in his thin, squeaky child's voice:

'Very well, my child, go and tell them to have everything ready. We shall come and officiate. Just make sure they make two or three pies with carrot filling for me, because I've had a certain weakness of the gut just recently. And what about Vasily Safronych himself – has he come home yet?'

'Not yet.'

'Well, there's nothing to be done. We'll have to get along without him. Just make sure the pies are ready, and we'll manage well enough . . . Oh yes, one more thing . . . tell them to have a large towel ready, because in this case I'll be dipping my biggest cross in the water.'

Yegorka returned as quick as a flash, and even cocked a snook at the devil as he passed the skylight window. What is more, the whole family had cheered up a bit: they had decided it would not be too great a hardship to get through just one more night, and that to make it less spooky, they would all go to bed in the same room – except that Yegorka agreed to keep Marfutka company in the kitchen, so that she shouldn't be frightened when she got out of bed in the night to turn the dough. The dough, which had been stood on the side of the stove and covered with a fur coat, was already warming and rising very nicely indeed.

During this time the devil had gone very quiet, as though sensing what was in store for him. He didn't play a single dirty trick on any member of the household that day. One or two people did say they heard him making a sort of snuffling noise: and then, as night drew on, bringing with it a hard frost, it seemed as though he was making groaning noises, and his teeth were chattering. This noise went on all night, and was heard by Marya Matveyevna and everyone else who happened to wake up for a time – but no one was particularly alarmed. Pausing only to mutter 'Serves him right, the Antichrist!', they crossed themselves, turned over, and went back to sleep.

Alas, this display of *sang-froid* was somewhat premature, and so enraged the evil spirit that at the very moment when the bell of Father Flavian's church rang out for the third time to summon the faithful to morning service, an extraordinarily doleful moaning sound came from Marya Matveyevna's attic, and at the same instant from the kitchen came the unaccountable noise of something crashing down and smashing to smithereens.

Marya Matveyevna leapt from her bed and, forgetting all fear, dashed down in her nightclothes to discover the cause of the commotion. When she saw the devil's latest piece of skulduggery, she froze in astonishment.

Standing in front of the stove, on which the dough had been stood to rise in a large earthenware pot, was Yegorka. He was smothered from head to toe in the dough, and surrounded by bits of broken pot.

Marya Matveyevna herself, Yegorka, and the hired woman Marfutka, who was sitting on top of the stove with her legs dangling down, were all so baffled by what had occurred that they shouted in one voice: 'God damn you!'

Thus with this evil omen the day began – the day on which we were destined to witness the outcome of Father Flavian and Deacon Savva's battle against the mysterious being which had raised a racket in the attic, and had now had the cheek to tip from the pot all the dough for the priests' pies.

And when had it done this? When it was already far too late to prepare a fresh batch of dough, and when the tall wiry sexton, carrying a heavy tinware bowl, was already rattling the iron ring on the side gate.

What could be done now to mend matters and to avert catastrophe in an affair which had started badly enough, but threatened to finish even worse?

Frankly, all these goings-on were considerably more intriguing than the whole Pectoralis affair. And although they apparently had nothing at all to do with him, they were to have the most direct and decisive bearing upon his fate.

XXII

Marya Matveyevna was terribly upset by the accident with the dough: she had no idea how she was going to break the news to Father Flavian that there were no pies with carrot filling for him. She decided it would be best not to bother him with the news at least until such time as he had performed the blessing of the water. As a woman of sense and experience, she was a firm believer in the policy of wait-and-see: she was convinced that that great magician, time, could still come to one's aid even in a situation where assistance appeared to be beyond the realm of reasonable expectation. And so it happened: as soon as the priests arrived, the ritual was begun; and before the service was ended, things took such an unexpected turn that there could be no more thought of pies with carrot filling.

What happened was this: the service was approaching its end, and Deacon Savva had just begun to intone the prayer for the prolongation of days, when an impatient knocking was heard on the still tightly locked attic door, and a somehow familiar but subdued voice was heard to say: 'Open up, let me out!'

Initially, need I say, this caused a bit of a stir, and everyone present made a terrified dash in the direction of Father Flavian . . .

When the door was opened, it was in truth an unexpected sight that met everyone's eyes: on the bottom step, framed in the doorway, stood none other than Safronych – or a demon that had assumed his guise. The latter seemed the more likely, particularly since, however cunning the disguise adopted by this spectre or devil, it did not entirely match the original. He was scraggier than Safronych for a start, with a deathly blue complexion and almost completely lifeless eyes. But what impudence! Undaunted by the sight of the *kropilo*, he went straight over to Father Flavian, held out his open hands, and offered them to be sprinkled with holy water – which Father Flavian promptly did. He then kissed the cross and turned casually to greet his family. Marya Matveyevna was obliged willy-nilly to acknowledge that this corpse-like figure was indeed her husband.

'Where on earth have you been, my duck,' she enquired, brimming over with sympathy and pity for him.

'Where the Lord put me for my sins, that's where I've been.'

'And was it you making those knocking noises?'

'I suppose it was.'

'But why were you hurling things about?'

'And why were you treating our little girl so badly?'

'And why didn't you come down by yourself?'

'Well, how could I, against God's will? . . . It was only when I heard the prayer for the prolongation of days that I decided to come down straight away . . . Make me some tea, good and hot, get me on to the stove and cover me with a sheepskin,' he muttered quickly in a hoarse, feeble voice. Aided by his wife and Yegorka, he clambered up on to the warm stove, where they wrapped him in sheepskins, while Deacon Savva went round the whole attic with his *kropilo* and discovered nothing of interest whatsoever.

As you will appreciate, after a revelation like that, there could no longer be any thought of sitting down to a good meal. Safronych's appearance in such a pitiful condition meant that the whole procedure had to be reduced on the spur of the moment to a bare minimum. Father Flavian made do with hot tea, which he took seated in a capacious armchair next to the stove, while Safronych thawed out and answered in desultory fashion a whole series of idle questions.

Safronych's understanding of recent events boiled down to his having been somewhere or other, clambered up somewhere or other, and found himself in hell, where he had had a long chat with Zhiga, who had disclosed that even Satan had tired of the quarrel between himself and Pectoralis, and that it was time to put a stop to it. Safronych had not dissented from that, but had decided to stay where he had been put for his sins: he had born it all bravely – the torture by cold and hunger, and the anguish of hearing his little daughter crying and moaning. Then suddenly he had heard the comforting sound of holy singing, and in particular the prayer for the prolongation of days, which he was very fond of; and when Deacon Savva chanted his name, he had suddenly fallen prey to other thoughts, and decided to go down once more, albeit briefly, to the earth, to enjoy Savva's singing and to bid farewell to his family.

That was about as coherent an account as could be got out of the poor fellow, and Father Flavian was in any case disinclined to press him further. His condition was truly pitiful: no matter how he shivered and tried to get warm, he couldn't manage to thaw out completely. Towards evening he became slightly more lucid and expressed the desire to have confession and prepare himself for death. A day later he died.

This all happened so quickly and unexpectedly that Marya Matveyevna, having scarcely recovered from the first trauma, now found herself making arrangements for her husband's funeral. This sorrowful task prevented her from paying due attention to the words of Yegorka, who had hurried off an hour after Safronych's death to order a coffin, and had come back with the strange news that 'the German had unblocked the gate to the yard of the old house' – the very gate, that is, that had caused the long dispute, and with it the undoing of both Safronych and Pectoralis.

With his enemy dead, Hugo was now able, without betraying his iron will, to open the gate and stop paying the ruinous indemnity – and that was what he had done.

He had, however, one more vow to keep: having outlived Safronych, he was bound to come to eat pancakes at his funeral – and that he also did.

XXIII

Scarcely had the clergy, the guests and Marya Matveyevna seen Safronych buried in the frozen graveyard earth and returned to the widow's new house to partake of the funeral feast, when the door was suddenly flung open to reveal, standing upon the threshold, the gaunt, pallid figure of Pectoralis.

No one was expecting him, so his appearance, quite naturally, took everyone aback, not least the grief-stricken Marya Matveyevna, who was at a loss to know how she should take it – as a sign of condolence or of mockery? Before she could select the appropriate response, Hugo Karlovich in a quiet, earnest voice, with all his customary self-esteem, informed her that he had come, in accordance with the solemn vow made some time ago to her late husband, to eat pancakes at his funeral feast.

'We're Christian folk: we turn no one from our door,' answered Marya Matveyevna. 'There's plenty of batter. We've made enough to feed an army of beggars, so you are welcome.'

Hugo bowed and sat down, what's more, in a place of honour, between the tubby Father Flavian and the stringy Deacon Savva.

Notwithstanding his somewhat haggard appearance, Pectoralis felt on top of the world: assuming the air of a conqueror, he conducted himself at the funeral feast of his enemy in a rather disgraceful fashion.

At this point a truly extraordinary thing happened to him, which admirably rounded off the story of his iron will.

I can't be sure how and why he got involved in an argument with Deacon Savva about that will of his, but the deacon said to him: 'Hugo Karlovich, brother, why are you for ever quarrelling with us and parading your will-power? You really shouldn't, you know . . .'

Father Flavian, coming to Savva's support, said: 'Indeed you shouldn't, dear brother; it's a sin for which you will be punished by God. God always punishes those who wrong us Russians.'

'Ah, but I outlived Safronych, didn't I? I said I would, and I did.'

'And what good has it done you? And for how long do you think you'll outlive him? The ways of God are inscrutable in punishing those who wrong us. Look at me: I'm an old man, I've no teeth, and my feet are so swollen I couldn't even squash a mouse – and yet maybe you won't outlive even me.'

Pectoralis merely smiled.

'What do you think you are grinning about?' the deacon intervened. 'Or have you lost all fear of God as well? Can't you see how skinny you've become? No, brother, you'll not outlive Father Flavian. You'll soon be kaput yourself.'

'We'll see about that.'

'What do you mean, "we'll see"? There's nothing more to see; you're already as shrivelled as a corpse. Now Safronych, he lived in his own simple way, and died likewise, enjoying himself as he knew best.'

'A fine way of enjoying yourself!'

'What was wrong with it? He lived out his days the way it pleased him – never short of a drink, and always ready to drink your health . . .'

'The swine!' said Pectoralis, unable to restrain himself.

'Oh, so he was a swine as well, was he? Why insult the man like that? If he was a swine, then let me tell you – he kept the fast up there in the attic just before his death, made his confession to Father Flavian, died like a Christian with his sins forgiven, and observed all the rites of the church. And maybe even as we talk, he is sitting chatting with his forefathers in Abraham's bosom, and telling them about you, and they're all having a good laugh. As for you – you're not a swine, oh no! You just sit and eat his food and besmirch his name. Now tell me, which of you is more a swine?'

'It's you rather, my dear fellow, that's the swine,' put in Father Flavian.

'He neglected his family,' Pectoralis responded coldly.

'What's that? What's that?' said the deacon. 'How do you mean, neglected? You just look around: whatever you say, he left his family a home and enough to live on. What's more, you're sitting in his house and eating his pancakes. But you, you've got no folk of your own, and when you die, you won't have two kopecks to rub together, there'll be nothing to pay for a funeral feast for you! So who took better care of his family? You should understand, brother, you can't get up to those sorts of nasty tricks with us, because we've got God on our side.'

'I don't believe that,' answered Pectoralis.

'Entirely as you please, but anyone can see it's better to die with a full larder like Safronych did, than perish from hunger like you're doing.'

Pectoralis was lost for words: he must have sensed the fateful significance of what the deacon had said. A sharp chill of terror ran through him, and Satan entered his soul, sneaking inside together with a pancake, which the deacon had offered him with the words:

'Here, have a pancake; eat it and keep quiet, because it's obvious you'll never keep up with us.'

'Who says I can't?' replied Pectoralis.

'Well just look at you, squashing it and cutting it and manducating it.'

'What does that mean – "manducating"?'

'What you're doing: chewing it and rolling it all the time from one side of your mouth to the other.'

'Aren't you supposed to chew them like that?'

'Why chew it? A pancake's as light as air – it slips down by itself. Take a look at Father Flavian over there, watch how he does it, see? It's a pleasure just to watch him. Look, pick it up by the edge, dip it well in sour cream, fold it up into a little envelope, then eat it whole, just as it is. Give it a little push with your tongue and let it slide down where it belongs.'

'It's not good for you, eating like that.'

'Tell us another one! I suppose you know better than everyone else! I'll tell you what, brother – you'll never eat more pancakes than Father Flavian.'

'I will,' replied Pectoralis gruffly.

'Let's have no boasting, please.'

'But I will!'

'Look, stop your boasting. You've just got out of one mess, don't rush into another.'

'I will eat more, I will, I will,' Hugo chanted.

So they made a wager – and since it could be settled there and then, the contest, to the pleasure of all present, began immediately.

Father Flavian had taken no part in the argument: he simply listened and went on eating. It was a match in which Pectoralis stood no chance. Father Flavian kept folding his pancakes into little envelopes and popping them down, with no sign of distress. Hugo's face flushed, then paled again, but he simply couldn't catch up with Father Flavian. The witnesses meanwhile sat around, watched and urged him on, to the point where Pectoralis should long since have packed his bags and made a run for it; but he had clearly never heard that discretion is the better part of valour. He ate and ate, until suddenly he slipped down beneath the table and began to snore.

Deacon Savva bent down and pulled him out.

'Now then,' he said, 'no malingering. Come on, brother – on your feet and tuck in. Father Flavian is still going strong.'

But Hugo made no attempt to rise. They went to pull him to

his feet, but he didn't budge. The deacon, who was the first to realize that the German wasn't pretending, gave his thigh a loud slap and shouted:

'Well, I'll be blessed! Here's a fellow who knew what sort of eating is good for you, and he's gone and died!'

'Died? Really?' said the company in one voice.

Father Flavian crossed himself, sighed, and whispering 'God is with us', moved another stack of hot pancakes within reach. So it came about that Pectoralis outlived Safronych by the tiniest margin and died in circumstances thoroughly inappropriate for a man of his character and intelligence.

He was buried hastily, on the parish, and, of course, with no funeral feast. None of us, his former colleagues, even knew about it. I, your humble servant, discovered what had happened quite by chance. On the day of the funeral I happened to go to town. The first snowstorm of the winter, but a really fierce one for all that, was raging. In a narrow sidestreet I encountered a coffin accompanied by Father Flavian, who was stumbling along in his fur hat and chanting the *Trisagion*. At that moment my sledge hit a snowdrift and one of the traces snapped. I got out and began to help the coachman, but it was a slow business, and while we were still at it, a woman in a padded jacket popped out through a rickety old gate, while another did the same on the other side of the street. They began to shout to each other across the street:

'Who are they burying then, ducky?'

The other replied:

'Eh, it wasn't worth coming out to see, my love. It's the German they're carting off.'

'What German is that?'

'You know, the one who choked on a pancake yesterday.'

'And is it Father Flavian who's burying him?'

'It's him, my love, it's him, the dear soul, Father Flavian.'

'God bless him!'

Whereupon the two women turned and slammed their gates shut.

Thus Hugo Karlovich met his end, and thus, and thus alone was he remembered – which, as it happens, I, who had known him in better times, with all his high hopes, found rather sad.

Notes

CHASING OUT THE DEVIL

Page 16: *Metropolitan Filaret's 'Catechism'* . . . Filaret Drozdov was Metropolitan of Moscow from 1821 until his death in 1867. His *Orthodox Catechism*, first published in 1823, was recognized as a standard exposition of the doctrine of Russian Orthodoxy.

Page 23: *Freiligrath's poem* . . . *Der Mohrenfürst* by Ferdinand Freiligrath (1810–76), the German romantic – and subsequently revolutionary – poet. Freiligrath was widely read in Russia.

Page 28: *the Vsepetaya icon*. An icon of the Madonna; literally 'The All-Glorified'.

Page 29: *the trepak* . . . a Russian folk dance, involving much stamping of the feet.

A SPITEFUL FELLOW

Page 34: *The Gostomelsky Farmsteads* . . . on the river Gostomlya in Orlov Province. This was Leskov's childhood home. Here, as often, Leskov weaves autobiography into his fiction.

Page 35: *nine versts* . . . A verst is a little longer than a kilometre: 1067 metres.

Page 37: *the 'mir'*. The village council, much revered by nineteenth-century Slavophiles as exemplifying the democratic instincts and institutions of the common Russian folk.

Page 43: *the local Invalid Company*. Local militia, made up of men invalided out of, or retired from, active army service.

A SHAMELESS RASCAL

Page 57: *Stepan Aleksandrovich Khrulyov* . . . General S.A. Khrulyov (1807–70), one of the heroes of the Crimean War, noted above all for commanding the valiant defenders of the famous Malakhov Kurgan in Sevastopol.

Page 57: *'chalked wins and losses on the slate, and never let the game abate'* . . . An inaccurate quotation from Pushkin's epigraph to Chapter 1 of *The Queen of Spades*.

Page 59: *'a pig in a skull-cap'*. Thus Khlestakov describes Zemlyanika in Gogol's *The Government Inspector*, Act V Scene 8.

Page 60: *Vaska* . . . The rascally Vaska, who listened calmly to the cook's remonstrations while continuing to lap the stolen cream, is one of the most famous heroes of the celebrated fables of Ivan Krylov (1769–1844).

Page 63: *Griboyedov commented upon that fact in his time* . . . So says Platon Mikhaylovich Gorich of Zagoretsky in Griboyedov's *Woe from Wit*, Act III Scene 9.

Page 63: *'The Russian Messenger'* . . . Katkov's journal *Russky vestnik* adopted, in the late 1850s, a profoundly anglophile stance.

Page 66: *Gogol's Petukh* . . . One of literature's more memorable gluttons; to be found in Gogol's *Dead Souls*, Part II.

THE ROBBER

Page 72: *Makary's fair*. Popular name for the annual Nizhny Novgorod trade fair, famous throughout Russia, which was held until 1817 in the town of Makarev. Makarev took its name from its monastery, the monastery of St Makary. Even after the site of the fair moved to Nizhny Novgorod (now Gorky), the event retained its old name in popular parlance.

Page 72: *a huge tarantass* . . . A tarantass was a sturdy four-wheeled carriage for country travel. Although passengers enjoyed some weather-protection in the form of a hood, the suspension was primitive, consisting of no more than two flexible longitudinal wooden members on which the coachwork was mounted.

Page 72: *'We don't care a toss for your complaint-book . . .'* Official complaint-books in Tsarist post-stations and railway stations caused as much mirth as do their equivalents in the restaurants, hotels, shops, etc. of modern Russia. Chekhov produced a hilarious set of imaginary extracts from such a tome in *The Complaint Book* (1884).

Page 73: *'according to the old belief'*. The 'Schism' which divided the Russian Church took place in the mid-seventeenth century. The schismatics, who rejected reforms in ritual, were known as 'Old Believers'.

Page 74: *a string of cracknels*. Small dry biscuits baked from wheat flour. The circular variety (*baranki*) mentioned here were carried threaded on a string.

Page 75: *had the luggage cut from the back of his carriage*. Luggage on a tarantass was carried in a trunk strapped on at the back. A stealthy thief could cut it away without alerting the passengers.

Page 77: *crossing himself with two fingers* . . . Old Believers (*see note on 'old belief', page 73 above*) crossed themselves with two fingers, not three.

Page 80: *kasha*. A staple Russian dish – a porridge, made from a variety of different cereal grains.

AN IRON WILL

Page 90: *Doberan* . . . Presumably a corruption of Dobbertin.

Page 109: *'God of the Mordvinians'* . . . The Mordvinians, a non-Slavic people dispersed throughout European Russia, retained – despite persecution and enforced russification – many of their ancient pagan beliefs.

Page 120: *'What the devil . . . at home.'* An extract from the popular song *When Mikheich thought to marry . . .'*

Page 120: *Sarepta* . . . A town in Saratov Province, founded by a community or *Herrnhuter*, or 'Moravian Brethren'. This religious sect, founded in Moravia in the eighteenth century, demanded of its adherents monastic standards of behaviour.

Page 121: *'The Miller's Wife from Marly'*. A French vaudeville, which enjoyed considerable success in Russia from the 1840s onwards.

Page 124: *Herrnhuter* . . . See note on Sarepta, page 120.

Page 124: *zakuski* . . . Those delightful and delicious cold snacks which Russians take with drink, or as a preliminary to a meal. *Hors d'oeuvres* would be a lamely inadequate translation.

Page 138: *Kizlyar vodka* . . . A grape-based vodka, produced in the town of Kizlyar in the Caucasus; very close to brandy.

Page 142: *'it was laid down . . . the lowest social order.'* The *ukaz* referred to was first published in 1871, and attributed to Tsar Aleksey Mikhaylovich (1645–76), who allegedly issued it in 1661. Almost certainly inauthentic, it would in any case be a red herring here: the word *nemtsy*, which now means 'Germans', would in 1661 have denoted all foreigners.

Page 146: *like the frog that wanted to look like an ox* . . . The hapless frog is the anti-hero of another Krylov fable.

Page 147: *'Prince of poets'*. Presumably Goethe ('Der Dichterfürst'), who died of a chill – though not, it should be said, as a result of falling drunk, into a ditch.

Page 167: *to stuff rags into the flue* . . . This quaint Russian habit reduced cold draughts when the stove was damped down for the night – and doubtless contributed to the numerous incidents of carbon-monoxide poisoning.

Page 173: *the holy gates* . . . The central doors in the iconostasis, or altar-screen, in a Russian church. Popular belief held that throwing them open could relieve cases of difficult childbirth.

Page 174: *kropilo*. A small brush, known in the Latin church as an aspergillum, used for sprinkling holy water.

Page 175: *kamilavka* . . . A tall purple velvet cap worn by Orthodox priests as a mark of merit, or distinguished service to the Church.

Also published by Angel Books

IVAN BUNIN
Long Ago
Selected stories translated by David Richards and Sophie Lund

FYODOR DOSTOYEVSKY
The Village of Stepanchikovo
Translated by Ignat Avsey

ALEXANDER PUSHKIN
The Tales of Belkin
with The History of the Village of Goryukhino
Translated by Gillon Aitken and David Budgen

ALEXANDER PUSHKIN
Mozart and Salieri
The 'Little Tragedies' translated by Anthony Wood

AFANSY FET
I Have Come to You to Greet You
Selected poems translated by James Greene
with essays by Henry Gifford and Yevgeny Vinokurov

In preparation

VSEVOLOD GARSHIN
From the Reminiscences of Private Ivanov
and other stories translated by Peter Henry and Liv Tudge

JOHANN WOLFGANG VON GOETHE
Torquato Tasso
Translated by Alan Brownjohn

LUDWIG TIECK, HEINRICH VON KLEIST
and E.T.A. HOFFMANN
Five German Romantic Tales
Translated by Ronald Taylor